STEPHANIE ERICKSON

THE FATE

CHILDREN of WISDOM · BOOK 1

ISBN-13: 978-0-9909293-8-3

The Fate is in your hands.

ONE

"The thread of life is a delicate thing. It is so easily broken. The Spinner must choose carefully when he plucks his materials from the dust, literally creating life from nothing." — Liv, Section 4, Paragraph 1: On Spinners

I stare into the darkness, searching for just the right bit of light. My orders come from higher up, so I already know who this man needs to be—calm, assertive, stern exterior with a soft interior. He'll make a good military man. All I have to do is get him started. The girls will help shape his life, and then we'll turn him loose on the world.

Finally, I see what I need. When I reach into the black cauldron, the silver mass clings to my hand as if I've just dipped it in cotton candy. I take it from the stone hearth over to the wheel, hook it onto the machine with the skill that comes from centuries of practice, and sit down to spin the man's life. When I'm finished, I pull the thread off the machine, a delicate silver line of light, and hand it to Horatia.

She smiles, carefully taking the thread from me and over to her desk. Desk is a loose term. It's more of a workbench really. Four wooden posts and a thick slab of wood make it look like an oversized cutting board. Our workspace is probably the most primitive in heaven, but it suits us. We're simple souls.

Horatia's straight, black hair tumbles down around her shoulders as she tips her head to the right, watching the light play against the thread, trying to decide how long it will take the man to fulfill his fate. I watch her, wondering how she always knows just where to cut.

"Don't sneeze," I call out, shattering our silent workspace. Galenia dissolves into laughter, but Horatia gives me a hot look that would melt steel.

Sheepishly, I smile and shrug, and Galenia composes herself in an admirable way.

Horatia goes back to the task at hand, and before long, her smile reappears as she brings her shears up and makes a clean slice in the thread, giving the man a nice, long life. I like the long ones. She hands the perfectly cut thread to the last of us, Galenia. She has the hardest job of all three of us.

Galenia's spot really does look like a desk. Whereas my other sister likes to stand as she works, Galenia prefers to sit, so her work surface is a bit shorter… A single candle sits in an ancient-looking brass candleholder with a looped handle just to her right, so she can easily reach it. To her left, she has a myriad of tools for fraying, cutting, burning, and otherwise damaging the ends of the carefully woven threads.

Galenia's brown hair falls in waves, and she tucks some of it behind her ears as she studies the man from her old, brown leather chair. She already knows what type of man he will be, what his life has in store for him, and how long he will live. Her job is to determine how he will die. She is a remarkably sweet woman, despite the fact that she constantly comes up with creative new ways for humans to die—from diseases to accidents. Needless to say, she's good at her job. But this man doesn't need a lot of fanfare. He will get to die old, surrounded by his family, in his bed. She holds the end of his thread over a candle, searing it so it won't fray, and that is that.

Another life complete.

I breathe a sigh of relief. We create so many different people that the normal ones are always a bit of a respite.

Webber's job is next, and he waits just outside our door to

complete it. Galenia hands the delicate thread to him, and the three of us watch as he carries it to the tapestry. He effortlessly weaves the new life into the fabric, until we can't tell where one stops and another begins.

He stands back, admiring his work, and we Fates do the same. The colors seem random up close, but as we step back, the larger picture becomes more and more apparent. The chaos turns to something beautiful. A never-ending garden landscape spread before us, growing more expansive with each life added.

"Life on Earth really is a beautiful thing," I say, putting my arms around my two sisters.

"The order comes down for a black thread. And not just any black thread, this one is meant to be the next Hitler. So black is his soul that the people on Earth will not even be able to see past his darkness. You are the Timekeeper. How long do you let him live?" Horatia asks from her seat between Galenia and me on the stark white couch in the common area.

There are lots of ways for heavenly workers to unwind here, but we prefer games. Someone plays a soft melody on the piano in the corner, while a few Keepers read on the other side of the room. Still others are mingling around, talking softly about the day's work.

Immediately, I know how I would answer. I'd snip that man's life so short that he'd never survive past infancy. His parents' pain would be a small sacrifice for protecting the rest of the world. It isn't my turn, though. We often play this game after hours—even the Fates need a break, after all—but Reapers usually never have the downtime to join us. Still, here Michaela sits, reclining rather calmly in an armchair on the other side of the coffee table, and we all hold our breath as we await her response.

She is a vision of a woman, and a typical angel. Long, blonde hair, beautiful blue eyes, and a sparkling smile to match. She has the ability to set a soul at ease with a simple glance. As a Reaper, she has a different understanding of humanity than we Fates do, which makes her an unpredictable addition to our game. Our decisions are made in the comfort of our workroom, but Michaela understands the consequences of those decisions in a very real way. She's walked the Earth; she knows what it's like to take a child from a parent's arms. She also knows what it's like to usher a soul through the gates of hell.

I hold my breath as I wait for her answer. She narrows her eyes, chewing her bottom lip as she considers. "That sounds like a rock and a hard-place scenario if I've ever heard one." Even her voice is angelic, as if the heavens are singing when she speaks.

Webber snorts. "What's the big deal? Black threads are the most fun." He examines his fingernails as he sits with one leg crossed over the other in his own armchair to Michaela's left.

I bristle as Webber reminds me of one of the many reasons I just don't care for him.

Before I can respond, Michaela turns her head and looks at Webber curiously, without a shred of judgment in her eyes. "Why?"

"Because they add contrast to the tapestry. All light colors would make it dull. The dark brings balance."

"So you don't think the world could ever be perfect? At peace?" she asks.

"The world *is* perfect," Webber answers simply.

Michaela smiles at his answer. I know light can only exist if there's darkness; otherwise, it would be impossible for us to discern either one of them. Still, I don't like Webber's know-it-all response. And I think there's more darkness in the world than there needs to be for humans to see the light. I'd like to think they're smarter than that.

Webber grins slyly at me, as if gloating about his victory. Wishing my deep blue eyes could turn him to ice, I stare at him and rub my constant five o'clock shadow of a beard.

"Fine then, Weaver," I say. "You think you've won the round. You ask the next question."

But Galenia, ever the peacemaker, speaks up, her soft voice cutting through the building tension. "You know that's not how the game works, Penn. It's Michaela's turn."

However, Michaela stares off into the distance with a blank expression on her face, and we all sigh at once, knowing the excitement of the game is over. She's getting another assignment.

"I'm sorry, guys. I have to go. Duty calls."

"Some day, you'll have to finish a round with us, Michaela," I say.

"I look forward to it," she says, smiling at me over her shoulder as she walks away, her black-and-white gown flowing behind her.

"I love it when she plays with us," Horatia says with a sigh.

"It certainly brings another perspective into the game," Galenia adds.

"It's not much of a game with just the Fates. I'll go see if I can find someone else to play with us," Webber says as he stands up.

"Nah, that's all right. If it's all the same to you, I'm done for now," I say, uninterested in spending any more time with Webber.

"Past your bedtime?" Webber asks.

"I've had my allotment of time with *you*, if that's what you mean," I say. I know it's rude, but I can't help it. He just rubs me the wrong way. Always has.

"*Penn*," Galenia scolds, and I can't help but shrink away from her, feeling like I just got my ears boxed.

"No, that's all right. He's just cranky because he knows I'd be better at his job than he is." A hush falls over the group. Webber is always jockeying for my job, just waiting for me to make a mistake. It feels like a constant battle.

Originally created by God to maintain Earth's birthrate, the first three Fates, and the many that followed, were all women. I'm the first male Fate. *Ever*. I didn't even start out as a Weaver like some Fates do to get their feet in the door. I was groomed all along to be a Spinner, as if God had hoped to purposely shake things up a bit by adding me to the mix. But others didn't see it that way. I was an outsider, a threat. Because of that perception, I've needed to prove myself over and over again.

Though no one outright says it, men are thought to be ill-equipped for our line of work, which requires compassion and motherly instincts—qualities more commonly attributed to women. But, much to Webber's chagrin, I'm awesome at my job. Many centuries have passed on Earth during my tenure. Webber's been waiting for almost as long to take it from me, but there are only three Fates at any one time, so he will just have to keep waiting.

I stand, stretch, and scratch my head, rumpling my already-messy mop of blond curls. "I guess we'll never find out, will we?"

"Never say never," Webber says to my back as I walk away. I try to let it just roll off, like water off a duck, but I fail... *again*. Just who does Webber think he is?

Here I am, one of the best Spinners in the history of the Fates, with no plans of leaving my post, but Webber keeps going at me. He can't get it through his thick head that I'm around to stay. Fates don't have a forced retirement age. We stay as long as we are useful, and not a moment more.

Horatia catches up to me just as I'm rounding the corner to my quarters. "Hey, don't let him bother you. He's just a Weaver."

"I don't hate him because he's a Weaver, Horatia. I hate him because he's always trying to edge me out of my job." I sigh. "He's actually a pretty good Weaver. He'd probably be a good Spinner, though don't tell him I said so."

"How did you start out again?" Horatia asks as we continue on down the dark hall. The walls are painted black, and the sky shines through the ceiling, displaying the glowing, shimmering galaxies that make up the heavens. The floor is dimly lit to prevent us from tripping, but we don't really need that feature. We've made the journey enough times to do it with our eyes closed.

"I got lucky. The sister whose place I took was ready to go. Fia, that was her name." The memory of her tickles the back of my mind. "I started spending time here before I was old enough to officially start working. I just couldn't keep myself away. My fingers itched to spin. Fia said I had a rare gift, so she never kicked me out. I think the other two hoped she would. I heard one of them say the creation process wasn't a spectator sport. Fia would just hush the naysayers with a wave of her arm. She's the one who taught me how to spin." I chuckle. "This one time, she told me sometimes you need a son of a bitch to spice things up a little. At the time, it shocked me, but now I know exactly what she means."

"So is Webber adding some spice to your life?" Horatia asks as we arrive at my quarters.

"I suppose so." I mean for it to come out lighthearted, but I say it through my teeth, making it sound like I begrudge the comment. Maybe I do.

"Whatever happened to Fia?"

"You know, I'm not sure. Once I took her post, she stopped by once or twice to see how I was doing. But I didn't see her again after that. She never talked about what she was planning to do." I shift my weight as Horatia leans against my doorway. I don't like not knowing what happened to my mentor. I've just been so busy and committed to the job that it never occurred to me to wonder. She helped me get my start. Because of her, I didn't have to fumble through my first few weeks on the job. I already knew what I was doing. How could I not know what happened to her? Why hadn't I tried harder to stay in touch?

"What happened to the one you replaced?" I ask.

"I don't know. I never even met her actually. You would've known her better than I did." Horatia's black hair bounces as she shrugs her shoulders.

I think back. Fia's sisters hadn't accepted me before I became a Fate. So once I was one of them, they isolated me further. I think it was mostly because I was male, but they never would've admitted that. So I kept to myself until Galenia came on board.

"In those early days, I stayed focused on my work, so I didn't talk much to the other two. They left not long after Fia did, anyway. I mean, Galenia took up her post only a few decades after I started mine. You weren't far behind."

I can't help but wonder what happened to them—what will happen to *me* once Webber finally succeeds in taking my place.

Horatia must notice the expression on my face, because she puts a hand on my shoulder. "Don't worry. I'm sure they're enjoying their retirement by now."

I nod, hoping she's right. Maybe I'll go see a Keeper tomorrow, find out what happened to them. Keepers hold the answers to all the questions in the universe, although they don't often share those answers. It might still be worth asking. Perhaps knowing that someone knows will be enough, even if I don't get exact details.

"Good night, Penn. I'll see you in the morning," Horatia says, adjourning to her own quarters.

"Night, Ratia." I walk to the end of my room and stare out at the heavens around me. A riot of stars, darkness, and light play against the canvas in front of me. After our conversation, I can't help but wonder—*what is the fate of the Fates?*

TWO

In the morning, I try to put my dark thoughts behind me. I stride to our workstation without allowing myself to be distracted by Webber, who leans against the wall of the weaving room, chewing a piece of straw.

I have purpose. I come, I spin life, and together, we populate the Earth. There isn't anything beyond that. There doesn't need to be.

"Ladies," I say as I walk into our room.

They smile and nod at me from their stations, ready to work. I walk over to the far wall, next to the cauldron, and take the first order of the day. Each new order appears after a completed one has been placed on the spike. Each spiked order disappears while we're making the new one. I've tried to catch the exact moment they disintegrate, but I've never been successful. I'm always too busy spinning.

This life will be an artist to balance the overly logical world. Creative, loving, and free spirited—that's what the world needs. Their fate is up to you.

—G

"Why does He sign the orders 'G'? Is He trying to be cool?" I ask as I approach the cauldron with the slip of paper. "Like, hey, G-money, what's going on?"

Galenia giggles. "I don't know. Maybe He doesn't have time to write the last two letters?"

"Hasn't He always done that?" Horatia asks.

"As long as I can remember," I answer.

"So why question it now?"

I peer into the dark cauldron. "I seem to be full of questions lately."

It takes some time to find the right materials. I lose track of how long I stand there, staring into the pot, waiting for what I need. Some days, it comes easily, and we can do hundreds of thousands of lives, keeping up with the growing demand of the expanding population of Earth. As I stare into the darkness, I realize today is not going to be one of those days.

The girls know better than to push me. I have earned my reputation as one of the best Spinners in history for a reason. I know what I'm doing, and so they wait patiently—Horatia sharpening her blades, and Galenia staring off into the distance, clearly daydreaming. She does this so frequently that someone who didn't know better would think she's spacey. I often wonder what she daydreams about. Even though she's the one who decides how the lives we create will end, I know she's too sweet to be dreaming of death.

I smile to myself as I watch her vacant expression. When I look back into the cauldron, the life is there. I reach in and pull out everything I need to create her, a pink mass of glittering wonder. As I turn her over in my hands, she shines iridescently against the low light of our room. Even Horatia gasps at the sight of her.

I carefully attach her to the wheel and begin my work. An actor, that's what she will be. And a singer, with the most beautiful voice the world has ever heard. This strand I'm creating speaks to my heart in a way I've never experienced. She will work on Broadway. She will make it big. Her life will be perfect in every way possible.

To my disbelief, I start to see her in my mind's eye. Normally, I never get a detailed picture of the people I create—I only know the basics of who they are and what they are meant to do. Their appearance is irrelevant. But this one shows herself to me. Her green, almond-shaped eyes look at me as if they truly see me. Her brown hair with natural blonde highlights will make her stand out among any crowd, as will her full, pouty lips—ones that I could kiss forever.

I shake myself as I spin her thread. I can't kiss a human. Fates and humans don't interact. *Ever.* Fates live in the heavens, and humans live on Earth. That is that. Without watching the humans we create, we wouldn't know how to equip them for their lives, but we *never* interact. It shakes me to feel this desire for a human, particularly since I've never felt this way about anyone *ever.* Attraction is a foreign concept for most heavenly souls. It's a very human emotion, and it's just not something that tends to happen to us. Feeling it now throws me off in a big way.

I fight the urge to sit back and analyze what it means. If I don't finish, her life will be incomplete, and I can't let that happen. Not to her. Taking a deep breath, I double down to complete her thread, knowing I've given her the best life I've ever bestowed upon any human. She will not know the dark side of fame. She won't struggle with addiction, won't be cheated on, or get a divorce. Her children won't die before her. Her life will truly be charmed.

As I hand her thread to Horatia, I know she won't cut it short. It's too lovely a thread. And, indeed, she does the life justice, leaving it one of the longest threads I've ever seen.

Once she's done, she hands it to Galenia, who gives it an almost wistful look. "My job seems pointless, doesn't it? Her life is so beautiful. It doesn't matter how it ends, because she will have *lived.*"

My throat closes as tears well in my eyes. I'm caught off-guard by the sudden onslaught of emotion. I cough to try and clear my head, then stand up a little straighter to watch Galenia work. The woman will die softly, passing into the night in her sleep. A perfect ending to a perfect life.

A collective sigh escapes us when Galenia is done, leaving

the tip of the thread perfectly rounded, not scorched or frayed at all like some.

"Magnificent." We're all starting so intently at the string that I don't even register which one of us said it.

Carefully, Galenia carries it to Webber, and the three of us watch him weave the new life into the tapestry. He's a skillful Weaver, but no matter what he does, she stands out against all the other threads, shining more brightly than the rest. But Webber doesn't seem to mind.

"Some people just don't fit in," he says as he stands back. "And look what a sparkling beauty she is. Well done, guys."

I shake Webber's hand at the genuine compliment. He may be gunning for my position, but he's not above appreciating a job well done. I can respect that.

"Now, when I start spinning, these little sparklers won't be such a rarity, I think," Webber says, shattering the moment.

My hand halts mid-shake. "But I thought you preferred the black souls." My voice is dark and low as I struggle to hold back the malice I feel toward Webber.

"I can appreciate all the threads on some level." The smug grin stays plastered on his face, making me bristle even more.

Horatia sighs. "Come on, Penn. There's more work to be done." She pulls at my shoulder, and I reluctantly break my stare-off with Webber to follow her back to our workroom.

"Why do you antagonize him like that?" Galenia, who's stayed behind, whispers to Webber. It's obvious she's trying to keep their conversation private, but I can hear every word.

"I'm only telling him the truth," Webber answers.

Galenia loudly sighs. "The very fact you believe that tells me, and everyone else, who is *actually* right for the job."

He doesn't say anything, so I look over my shoulder to gauge his reaction. Webber is standing up a little straighter as she walks away, and I can tell he has totally missed her meaning.

As we return to our stations, I can tell I'm not the only one having trouble moving past the pink thread. "I don't think I will ever top that," I say as I stare into the cauldron, watching the darkness swirl in a pot I never stir.

"No, probably not. But is that really what this is about? One life being better than another?" Galenia asks. I only realize she's behind me when she puts a soothing hand on my shoulder.

Horatia smiles broadly at me, indicating she agrees with our sister.

"No, I suppose it isn't," I say as I stare at the order lying on a table next to my spinning wheel. I have to spike it. But once I do, she's gone. It's a surprisingly difficult task for me, and I'm not sure I fully understand why.

With the other two watching me, I try not to look too stilted as I walk over to the spike on the wall by the hearth. I read her order one last time, savoring the words, remembering who she is. After, I stab it through, pushing it all the way down to the bottom of the spike.

The next order appears in its place on my table, and as I grab it, I can't shake the feeling that I've peaked. I've reached the top of the mountain, and it will all be downhill from here.

Downhill means easier, right? I think, trying to comfort myself as I read the next order.

Logical and even tempered, but also kind and compassionate.

—*G*

"This one's a short order. And it's another kind one. We're due for a doozy of a black thread soon. But until then, let's have some fun," I say as I set the order aside and peer into the darkness. I try to think of when we prepared our last truly black thread. We've had plenty of greys lately—souls capable of choosing either good or evil. The last truly black one was a while ago. In fact, enough time has passed that the man must be well into old age by now, if he's even still alive. He's probably incarcerated for his crimes, murdered by someone else, or in hiding. I don't remember how long his thread was. I try not to dwell on the black ones.

As I set the order down next to the wheel, I decide who this man will be. He will be for her. He will match her every step, her every need, and her every whim. He will balance her. Smiling, I put my hand into the cauldron and pull a blue lump of life out of the pot. It's not as special as the last one, but it will do.

The woman's eyes haunt me as I spin her true love's thread. That's probably for the best. Because she is so vividly in my mind as I create her match, their souls will connect on a deeper level.

When we're done with him, Webber skillfully finds his place, complementing our sparkler nicely.

As the day wears on, she continues to haunt me, and I find myself struggling to focus. We close out the day with an all-time low of threads produced.

We all know why, but no one says a word about it. In fact, we each go our separate ways when we're done, instead of adjourning to the common area for a game or some general relaxation like we normally do. Walking in silence to our quarters, we separate. We don't even say goodnight to each other.

As I shut my door behind me, I wonder how we will move on from her, how *I* will move on. The girls don't seem as affected by her as I am. They're obviously moved, but they did their jobs with little hesitation for the rest of our shift. But me… I find myself wondering what the point is now that someone so perfect has been created.

My room is pretty simplistic. I have everything I need, plus one or two things I don't. Immortals have no need for sleep, so I don't have a bed like the humans on Earth do. Instead, I have a very comfortable couch, which sits opposite a grand bookshelf filled with both heavenly and earthy writings, and my bathroom is next to that. The room is decorated in a stark white, causing the darkness of the night sky to stand out even more.

I settle down on the couch and stare up at the heavens. A meteor streaks across the ceiling, hurrying off to who knows where. As I watch it disappear into the darkness, I wonder if I just need some closure.

Getting up, I leave my room and pad across the hall, heading back toward our workroom. Only a few souls are still milling around, mostly Healers making their way to the common area, I assume.

Instead of going straight into the workroom, I head to the Weaver's room. My eyes automatically find her in the tapestry.

As I stand there, I watch her placed in her mother's arms for the very first time. Her parents know she is special. Kismet, they name her. It suits her. I watch the first few days of her life before returning to my room.

Time passes differently in the heavens than it does on Earth. It takes a year on Earth for a week to pass in the heavens. I find myself drawn to the weaving room each night to watch her grow. I know I'm not supposed to fixate on a single human this way. We're supposed to watch a variety of people, get a feel for their environment and the challenges they face. But I can't keep my eyes off her.

Galenia catches me in there a few times, but she says nothing judgmental. She even asks me how our little sparkler is doing, and I can tell she's genuinely curious.

The more I watch Kismet, the more my production suffers. I just can't seem to achieve the same volume of threads I once could. What's worse, I'm having trouble seeing the point. My heart is with Kismet.

I watch her for nearly six months, twenty-four years on Earth. She excels at almost everything, though that's not to say it's all easy for her. Where most would give up, she continues to struggle, refusing to entertain a single shred of doubt that she will achieve what she wants.

I remain glued to her life, watching as she moves to New York despite her parents' wishes. But their worries are unfounded. She blossoms, booking acting jobs while attending school on a nearly full scholarship. Somehow, through it all, she remains humble. Although she works hard, she will never experience real hardships or financial struggle. I did that on purpose, because I didn't want such a perfect creature to experience those things. I wanted her to shine, and shine she will.

Webber finds me standing there one morning, fixated on Kismet's thread.

"You're in here pretty early, Penn," he says.

"What time is it?" I ask, struggling to get my bearings. I let myself get carried away the night before.

"Time to start work, man. Get it together." He looks from me to the tapestry, then back again, and a wicked smile spreads across his face. "You were here for her again, weren't you?"

My eyes find her on their own accord. I stare at her, although I don't see her life anymore; all I see is her sparkling thread.

Webber laughs. "Oh, this is too perfect. I don't need to do anything. Just sit back and watch you destroy yourself over some *human*," he says.

My breath comes in short bursts as I recognize the truth of his words. Backing away from the tapestry, I head out into the hallway. Turning, I run into our workspace, crashing right into Horatia.

She falls back, knocking her shears off the table as she goes down. Her hands automatically go out to catch her fall, and she lands right on the shears. The super-sharp blades pierce her hand. Although we're all immortal, that doesn't mean we don't bleed when we run scissors through our hands. I rush over to kneel by her side just as Galenia walks into the room. Though she must be shocked by the sight of us—nothing like this has ever happened before in our workroom—her immediate reaction is to gather some cloth and bring it over. Time seems to move in slow motion as we wrap our sister's hand and take her to the Healers.

We wait outside in the stark white hallway while they work on Horatia. "I guess we won't spend the day making up for our losses yesterday, huh?" I ask, trying to make a joke, but the concern in my voice kills all hints of humor.

"No, I don't suppose we will." She stares thoughtfully down the long corridor of healing rooms. The heavens aren't particularly hazardous, so a lot of the rooms are actually used for human souls that are anchored somewhere between the heavens and Earth. People on Earth would say they're in comas. When they're in the healing rooms, they can rest while the Healers on both sides do their work. Some humans wake up from their comas, some don't—whether because they don't want to go back, they're too far gone, or they don't understand how to get back.

But it's rare for a heavenly body to need a Healer's services.

"What happened, Penn?" Galenia finally asks.

"I bumped into her, and she fell on the shears."

Galenia eyes me, and I know she knows there's more to it than that, but she doesn't press me. Instead, she nods and says, "When you're ready, I'll hear the rest of it."

I suck in a breath, and we sit in silence until a Healer comes out and breaks the tension. She's wiping her hands on a white cloth. It drapes down her front, not fully covering the blood-stain on her shirt. I cringe, knowing I was at fault for my sister's injury. I have no idea what will happen to me if I can't get it together, but I have a feeling I don't want to find out.

"She'll be fine. Should be totally patched up and ready to work tomorrow. All signs of the injury will be gone by then." Between the heavens' phenomenal Healers and an immortal's divine ability to recover, our sister should be back to normal in a day. On Earth, they'd call it a miracle. In the heavens, we call it necessary. Our work is never over.

Galenia smiles. "Thank goodness for that. Can we see her?"

"Of course." The Healer smiles comfortingly, as is their way, and ushers us in to see our sister.

Horatia is sitting up on a plush white bed, and her hand is out to the side, wrapped in silvery linens. All traces of blood have been wiped away.

Galenia lets out a sigh, as if she's been holding her breath since she last saw our fallen sister, and rushes forward to grab Horatia's good hand and hold it close.

"Jeez, Gale, I'm immortal. It's not like I was in any real danger," Horatia says.

"No, I know, but I think we were both worried about your ability to keep working."

Horatia turns a critical eye on me. "What happened?"

My eyes dart back and forth between the two women—my most-trusted companions, my sisters. "I don't know," I finally say.

Horatia and Galenia exchange a long look. "I think that's

the truth of it," Galenia says, "but whether he's too blind or scared to see it is up for debate."

Horatia rolls her eyes. "Penn, we all know how much that girl has gotten to you. She got to all of us back when you created her. But you have to move on. They're human. They lead their own lives. You know that."

I can't help but stare at her injured hand.

"Penn, maybe you should take a vacation," Galenia suggests. "Explore some of the galaxies, shadow a Reaper, do something else to take your mind off her."

"I'm sure Webber would be more than happy to fill in," I say, frowning at the prospect. "All he needs is an opportunity, and I won't be the one to give it to him."

"At what cost?" Galenia asks.

"Everything," I answer as I leave the girls alone in the healing room.

THREE

I lock myself inside my room, but I can't focus. I try reading a book, but it's as if her face is blocking the page. All I see is her. Her eyes, her face, her lips, her beautiful hair... I shake my head in an effort to clear it.

I need to walk. The halls are buzzing with the day's activity, but I can't register what's going on around me. Instead, I watch my feet as they move me along. I'm not surprised when I find myself in front of the Keepers' work floor.

I stand there for a moment, considering what to do. Kismet has so consumed me, I nearly forgot about my predecessors' fate. The Keepers might be able to give me some peace. Perhaps it will give me some closure about where my life is going. But will it be enough to help me get back on track? Resolved, I put my hand on the door. I have to try.

The room opens to shelf upon shelf upon shelf of books. Millions of volumes of information—the whole history of the heavens and the Earth is held within those walls. A half-empty shelf to my left is quickly being filled with new volumes flowing in from Earth—creative works, scientific ones, and chronicles of history. There are apprentices bustling around everywhere, shelving volumes and taking them down. There's some system of order, but I have no idea what it is. I make my way further into the room, staring up at the staggering height of the shelves as I pass them. I squint, trying to see the top, but it's too distant, even for eyes as sharp as mine.

Finally, I find myself in front of one of the Keepers. With a long, grey beard, wrinkled skin, gnarled hands, and a hunched back, he's an old man in appearance, which isn't unusual for Keepers. They feel like the aged hold more wisdom, and it does take centuries upon centuries to achieve Keeper status. Not all apprentices advance to that point. The elderly appearance, though completely voluntary, is a badge of honor of sorts.

He sits in an oversized leather chair situated between the towering cases. I'm not surprised to see there's a book in his hands.

"Well, to what do I owe this pleasure, dear Fate?" the Keeper asks in a voice that quavers under the weight of years gone by. He sets the enormous volume on a small table next to his chair, which I'm not entirely convinced can handle the weight of the book.

"I was hoping you could tell me what happened to the Fates who came before me." I shift my weight, suddenly nervous about what the Keeper may or may not say.

The Keeper narrows his gray eyes at me. "Why do you ask?"

"I was thinking of Fia the other day, the Spinner I replaced. She was a good friend, and the more centuries that pass, the more I wonder what happened to her."

"And what will happen to you," the old man fills in.

I nod. It's undeniable.

The Keeper sits back, causing his chair to creak in complaint. "My dear boy, you wish for something you don't even grant to the humans you create."

I search the man's face, trying to understand his words.

"You do not allow them to know their fate," he continues. "What makes you think you can handle yours?"

"Does a Fate even have a fate?"

The old man chuckles, his laughter flooding his whole face with joy, and I can't help but smile. "We all play a role in God's plan for this life, even the Fates."

"But what will become of me when I'm finished playing my role?"

"There's your mistake. You are never done. Think of Fia. You still remember her and use the techniques she taught you, do you not?"

I nod again.

"Then is she not serving her larger role, even though she no longer works among us?"

"Yes, I suppose she is. But, Keeper, we are immortal. Where did she go? And what is she doing now?"

The Keeper smiles as he tents his hands in front of his face. "She has moved on. Some might say to a better place."

When I hear his words, I immediately jump to conclusions. "But the very definition of immortal means to live forever. She died? How? When?" I become frantic; he seems to be confirming my worst fears.

"Death is something humans experience. Their bodies age, and eventually stop functioning, but their souls live on, as you well know. I suppose the concept is similar for us. Her soul has moved on from this place. Fia is at peace now. Knowing that, you should be too."

I take an unconscious step away from the Keeper. Part of me knows I will never experience peace again, not after seeing that girl. Not after discovering that Fia is no more.

Nonetheless, he has helped me. I hold a hand out to him. "Thank you, Keeper. I know your time is very valuable."

"Perhaps not as valuable as yours, Fate." The foreboding tone of his voice makes me pause. His eyes seem to slice into me.

"What do you mean?" I ask, still lightly grasping the old man's hand.

"I mean that your time may be shorter than mine. Be diligent, or you will soon meet your fate, and you may not like it."

The old man disappears right before my eyes, leaving me with my outstretched hand hanging in midair.

A chill runs down my back, but I do my best to soothe myself of the uneasy feeling. I already know things are spiraling out of control; I don't need an old man to tell me that. *Diligence.* How in the heavens am I supposed to be diligent, when I'm so consumed by Kismet?

The Keeper seems to think there will be some pretty dire consequences if I don't get myself under control. But how? And what if I don't want to control these feelings that are building up inside me? They're exhilarating and consuming. What would I give up to stay on this path with her?

As I wander back to my quarters, I have a feeling I will soon find out.

Before I make it back, I run into Michaela.

"Hello there, Penn. How nice to see you on this side of the heavens." I welcome her warm smile, which helps restore what remains of my shredded nerves.

She must notice the grim look on my face because her expression fades to concern. "Care to walk with me a bit?"

I fall into step beside her, giving her my answer without any words. For a few moments, we don't speak at all. My mind whirls like the contents of my cauldron as I try to decide how to begin... or if I even want to share my troubles with her. It feels a little like opening Pandora's Box. Once I admit everything out loud, there will be no going back.

Trying to think of something to lighten the mood, I decide to start a game with her. Given her love for the human world, I pick a song lyric. All she has to do is finish it. *"Wise men say,"* I venture.

"Only fools rush in." Michaela ponders for a moment as we walk. We have made our way to the observatory, where many of the immortals like to sit and watch the heavens. It's a beautiful place filled with stars, planets, and life.

Michaela turns her back to it all to face me. "You've fallen in love with her."

I don't respond right away. How can I deny it? Of course I have. How could I not? How could every single being—human or heavenly—who either saw her or met her *not* fall in love with her?

"How did you know?"

"Your sparkler is a real beauty. I've even stopped by the Weaving Room to see her." I can hear the smile in her voice as I watch the heavens. "How's Horatia?"

"Oh good. You heard about that too," I say, embarrassed.

"I did."

"She'll be ready to work again tomorrow."

She nods as we go, and then asks, "Why did you fate her for someone else?"

My mouth hangs open, and I know she isn't talking about Horatia. "Did I have a choice?"

Her smile is soft and a little sad. "There is always a choice. To live your life or waste it. Heaven or hell. To move forward or stand still."

Shaking my head, I try to understand what she's saying. I assume moving forward means forgetting Kismet, but if I do that, I'll be doing what I've always done, for as long as I can remember. I will be standing still.

"What—" I start to ask, but she puts a hand on my shoulder and smiles at me.

"I have to go. But before I do, consider this—the humans are beautiful and frightening. They are full of emotions that most of us don't understand or ever experience. Who wouldn't be curious about that? Perhaps the first step to moving forward is forgiving yourself."

Am I really so transparent? With that, she squeezes my shoulder and leaves me alone in the observatory. No doubt she's received an assignment.

I am a Fate, a heavenly being. I shouldn't be feeling this way about a human. But I have absolutely no desire to change, which makes me feel even worse. My focus has deviated from my purpose in a big way, making me feel lost—something I've never felt in the entirety of my long existence.

As I stare out at the heavens, not really seeing anything, I wonder if I can do what Michaela suggests. I wonder if I can forgive myself.

The following day, I am the last to arrive at our workroom. Thankfully, I'm so late that Webber is already in the weaving room, and I don't have to deal with him—not yet, anyway. I clear my throat as I walk in through the arch-shaped stone doorway. "Horatia, I'm truly sorry for my carelessness yesterday. It won't happen again."

"Penn, it's all right. I'm fine," she says as she assesses me. "It's you we're worried about."

"I'm just as fine as you are. Now, let's get to work," I say, trying to end the discussion.

I don't miss the look Horatia and Galenia share, but I let it go. It's Michaela's words that won't leave me in peace. Am I moving forward or standing still? I want to move forward, but I just don't know how. Sighing, I grab the next order and set to work.

But I'm agitated. I've never felt this kind of pressure before. When I first started, I had nothing to lose, so I had no point of reference when it came to stress. Anyway, stress is typically a human emotion. But as I stare down into the blackness of the cauldron, it feels as if I'm split in two. I know I have to keep working, that I have to move past her, but I don't see how I can. I don't want to. Moving past her means giving her up, right?

One thing is certain—I can't go on this way. My production over the last six months has been terrible. I went from being the best Fate in history to the worst overnight. It has to stop. Whether I choose to move forward or stand still, I need to choose something. It's hurting everyone. Horatia and Galenia have become anxious as rumors about our poor production have spread throughout the heavens—helped, no doubt, by Webber. On Earth, a new generation of career-minded women is being blamed for the current low birth rate, but I know that won't last forever. Things will start crumbling if I don't pick up the pace.

I will move forward, I think, although I'm not yet sure if that means letting go of Kismet and focusing on work, or focusing on Kismet and letting go of work.

Trying to silence the questions in my mind, I hastily reach into the pot and pull out a muddled, brown mass. Someone's breath hitches as the light hits the raw material, but I don't know which of the girls made the sound. I don't look up to find out. I'll show them I can still do the job—without giving up Kismet.

I slap the mass onto the wheel and start working, but it isn't right. No matter what I do, I can't spin much of anything from the muddled mess. The more I struggle with it, the more frustrated I get. As the day ticks away, the new pressure I feel weighs heavier and heavier on me.

Finally, after struggling for hours with the mass, I have a thread. But I can't see the life inside it at all. Trying to ignore the obvious, I pull it off the wheel and hand it to Horatia.

She takes it from me gingerly, but then she immediately recoils. "Penn, this thread…" She trails off, and I look nervously from her to the thread, knowing that somehow I managed to tie my own fate to that thread.

She picks up her shears and cuts it terribly short. It's not even an inch long. No wonder I can't see the human inside the thread. There isn't much to see. I created a stillborn by mistake. My breathing comes in short gasps as Horatia hands the thread to Galenia. I reach for it instinctually, but Galenia gets to it first.

"Penn, it's over. It's done. There's nothing for him now," she says, referring to the baby. A him. A life cut short because of me. Galenia carries the thread toward the door.

I step in front of her before she can leave our room. "Please. Not Webber," I say in an undertone. "This is just the opportunity he's looking for."

With tears in her eyes, she moves around me and says, "Then you shouldn't have given it to him."

Horatia stays back with me as Galenia walks alone toward Webber.

"It's about time," I hear Webber say. "What is this? A stillborn? There weren't any orders for one today."

Galenia's silence is all the confirmation he needs. "It's a mistake. The great Penn has made a mistake! Finally." He pushes past Galenia and runs down the hall, not even bothering to gloat in front of me. He's going straight to our boss with my mistake. And I know that's where it will end.

FOUR

We gather in the workroom, not sure what to do. Huddling close together, we don't speak, our arms encircling one another's shoulders, our heads bowed together in the center of our circle. The girls' hair dangles down into the middle, occasionally tickling my knees, but I ignore it. This is my family. I can't imagine being parted from them. This is what I should've thought about instead of Kismet. But as soon as the thought is in my head, I regret it. Why should I have to choose one or the other? It's not fair.

Michaela bursts into the room, interrupting our huddle. The outright fear in her eyes makes my heart race. "Guys, I think we have a problem," she says.

But before I get to hear what she has to say, the archangels come for me. "Penn, come with us," they say when they arrive at the door. They are blond and blue eyed like Michaela, but much, much bigger, and swathed in white robes.

Michaela looks back and forth between the angels and me, confusion on her face. "What's going on?"

But I can't explain. They're waiting. I nod to the angels, knowing there's no use fighting them. Anyone who tries will lose, and lose quickly.

The girls follow closely behind, well, as closely as you can follow a couple of archangels. Their massive, stark-white wings are so enormous that they force those around them to give them a fair amount of space on either side and behind. They are fore-boding by design. I wonder if it's a lonely existence, but before I have much time to think about it, we arrive at our destination.

Michaela stands a few paces behind my sisters, her face drained of all its remaining color. What she said nags at my mind. She didn't know about my mistake. So why's she so wor-ried? What could have happened? But the archangels are breath-ing down my neck, so I don't get a spare moment to ask.

Webber is leaning against the wall next to the door, smil-ing widely. We lock eyes, and a gamut of emotions washes over me—anger, defeat, and denial are the most prominent. But I can tell Webber feels only glee. It makes my frown furrow even deeper. I can only hope Webber won't be as bad in my position as I fear he will be. But the scenarios start playing in my head on their own accord. I picture Webber making the tapestry's threads darker and darker, ruining the fragile balance of Earth. And I worry that my sisters will be miserably unhappy with someone as arrogant as Webber at their helm.

I glance back at them once more before I'm ushered into the office of God. The looks on their faces mirror the way I feel—dark, concerned, and depressed.

Inside, everything is white. There appears to be no defini-tion between air and floor; it's just a sea of white all around me. My shoes make a sound as I walk, so I know I'm connecting with some kind of ground.

Soon, though, shapes start to take form in front of me. First, a chair materializes, then a great podium facing it, buffeted by several smaller podiums on either side. God sits in a chair be-fore the tallest podium, and some of His disciples have assumed similar positions at the smaller ones around him. I've never met God before. I've never had a call to. I immediately regret meet-ing Him under these circumstances.

"Fate, please, have a seat," He booms.

I obey automatically, and the angels stand on either side of me. "You know I'm not going anywhere, right? It's not like you have to stop me from running away or something," I whisper to them. But they don't respond. They stare stoically ahead. And why wouldn't they? Their heads aren't on the chopping block.

I venture a good, long look at our creator. He isn't an old man with long, flowing gray hair. And He isn't a young, bearded Middle Eastern man either. He's relatively young looking, perhaps middle-aged by Earth's standards. He has short, dark hair, and wears steel-rimmed glasses and a button-up blue checked shirt with no tie. He must like the current fashion trends on Earth, because I can't imagine he needs the glasses. He's God.

He looks down at something on His podium, and I can only assume it's the thread I created. My mistake.

"You've made a mistake," God proclaims.

I don't respond. I have no rebuttal for that. It's the truth, plain and simple.

The creator takes off his glasses and rests them on the podium in front of Him. "Have you truly nothing to say for yourself?" He asks, looking straight at me.

The more I think about it, the less I can answer him. I have no excuses. I can neither explain nor defend my behavior. I myself don't understand it. I feel human emotions, so many of them, and yet I'm not a human. How can I put that into words? I can't. So, I sit and await his judgment.

God frowns at me, making me long for an excuse that would help me escape His disapproval. "Penn, you are the best Fate our world has ever seen, but you have just made one of the worst mistakes a Fate can possibly make. Due to your inept creation, a life has needlessly been cut short. You have offered no excuse or explanation for your error." God pauses, waiting for me to disagree, but I can't.

The only thing I can do is apologize. "I'm sorry. I truly don't understand what's come over me."

The creator sighs. "Be that as it may, I cannot allow the unnecessary loss of life to go unpunished. It is with the deepest regret that I sentence you, Fate, to banishment. You are to live out the remainder of your existence on Earth, never to see or interact with the heavens again. You will however, remain immortal. You will not be allowed to escape your banishment by dying. You will wander the Earth forever."

My mouth hangs open as I try to process my harsh sentence. Banished? How many others have been banished? Of course, there are those the humans refer to as fallen angels. But that was eons ago, during the formation of the Earth. Are there even any left?

I clear my throat. "I didn't know you still practiced banishment."

"In this case, I think it's a suitable solution. You have a long history as a Fate, and you're the best we've had so far. Such an achievement does not go ignored. However, you seem suddenly unfit for the work. I don't mind telling you that you will be missed." There's a strange emotion in His eyes when they meet mine—something like hope. "Take heart. You may find yourself very useful on Earth. I'm not through with you yet, Penn."

My breath catches in my throat. Does he really have a larger plan for me? Or will I be making my own fate from here on out?

Either way, I know instinctively that this will be the last time I ever hear the voice of God.

FIVE

The archangels lift me firmly, but not roughly, from my seat and usher me out.

A line of my friends, coworkers, and acquaintances has assembled on either side of the hallway. Word of my expulsion has apparently traveled fast. I spot Webber first, and he starts to clap as I walk past him. No one else joins his attempted chorus, so his clapping echoes solemnly, almost chasing me as I go.

I see Horatia and Galenia next. Both have tears in their eyes. I try to go to them, wanting to at least tell them goodbye, but the archangels hold up their hands in a clear signal. My sisters and I share a long look, knowing it will be the last time we'll see each other.

I wonder what will become of them, and how they'll function with Webber in my place. Horatia doesn't much care for the guy, but Galenia always tries to find some good in those around her. And who will replace Webber as the Weaver? Down and down the dominos fall as my one mistake ripples through the heavens and Earth.

Michaela catches my eye last. Unsaid words hang on her lips. She knows better than to come to me, but the desperation on her face makes me think she'll try. She doesn't though, and I lose sight of her before I have the chance to hear her out, which makes my departure unsettling to say the least.

Once we leave God's office, I am not allowed to return to my quarters or our workroom. I don't need any of my heavenly belongings where I'm going. We don't even walk back through the areas I know best. I don't get to see the common area or the observatory. Once the crowd thins and fades away, we're left in the mists, and I know we're nearing the edge of the heavens.

Soon, the mist becomes so dense that I can't see in front of me anymore. Waving a hand in front of my face to try to clear the air, I stop walking.

"Keep moving," one of the archangels behind me says. They are working together as a single unit, so I have no idea who made the command.

I hesitate, fear starting to slow my steps, but I feel the angels push me forward.

"Fate, do not fear this moment. We are with you now." Their voices are deep and terrifying, but I can tell that in their own creepy way, they're trying to soothe me.

Knowing I have no choice, I continue to put one foot in front of the other and march blindly toward my future.

After what feels like an eternity of walking, I arrive at the end of the mist. I find myself standing at the edge of a cliff, somehow looking down at both the heavens and at Earth. I'm not ready—not remotely.

"Godspeed to you, Fate," the angels say together as the ground beneath me disintegrates… and I fall.

The fall is like nothing I've ever experienced. The rush steals my breath away, but as my body begins to adjust, I start to absorb what I'm seeing below me.

At first, there's only darkness, but then, I see a brilliant light. Soon, the earth is revealed to me in all its beauty. I see the clouds—including a hurricane over the Gulf of Mexico—the continents, and the oceans. I see my new home in all its glory, and the sight brings tears to my eyes. It's impossible to deny all I am losing, but I will be gaining so much too.

I lose all concept of time as I fall, and my mind starts to wander.

What will happen if I land in the ocean? Would it be better than landing on the ground? Will the impact kill me? The Keeper implied I could die, but God also said I would wander the Earth forever. I tend to believe God over the Keeper. So, I will survive, but what kind of existence will I have? As Earth looms larger and larger beneath me, I realize I'm about to find out.

I come crashing down in the swamps of Florida. As I watch the peninsula grow larger and larger as I approach, I land right in the middle of the Everglades with a thunderous crash. The water and muck spray out around me on all sides, creating a crater that quickly fills in with water and slime. I've been left with nothing. No money. No transportation. No food. Nothing but the shimmering gold robes of a Fate, which will look ridiculous on Earth. To make matters worse, I've landed in knee-deep water, and the robes are already soaked through to my skin. I take a step forward, more to keep myself from getting stuck than anything else. I have no real direction just yet.

A gator swims past me, but I don't feel any fear. If anything, I'm fascinated to see one in the flesh. The novelty wears off quickly, though, and my dire situation starts to sink in, much as I continue to sink into the muck. I don't try to walk any further. In fact, I sit back and let the water soak me up to my armpits.

The isolation and desperation I feel sitting there in the swamp threatens to overwhelm me. Michaela's face and her problem flash in my mind, giving me a brief sense of urgency, but the muck of self-pity quickly smothers it.

"What's the point?" I say out loud. There's nothing I can do to help her. I am beyond offering or receiving help. I could sit here until the end of time and watch the whole world die around me. I've been banished. I feel humiliated. I am a Fate, but I've been reduced to sitting in a swamp with nothing to live for. All because of Kismet. *Kismet.*

A thought occurs to me. I'm on Earth. With her. I could

find her.

I have no idea how much time passed while I was falling. Time passes so much more quickly on Earth than it does in the heavens. When I stopped watching her, she was in her twenties, just about to meet her true love. The thought makes me stand up straight, creating a splash of water that startles some of the wildlife around me.

Will I interfere with her fate? Can I? What do I expect her to say if we meet? She won't love me. Not in a million years. I know this because I'm the one who created her perfect love. So what would I even hope to accomplish by meeting her?

I let my head fall back to watch the clouds float above me, a true marvel to behold.

Closure, I think. I can have closure.

Several problems are staring me in the face at the moment, the most immediate one being that I'm stranded in the middle of a swamp. I look in all directions, searching for some kind of indication of civilization, some possible savior. All I hear are the sounds of the swamp—cicadas, frogs, and an occasional splash in the water. Nothing helpful. It's so blasted sunny out that I can't even navigate by the stars. The sun is to my left, but is it rising or falling? Before I can get too frustrated, I hear a mechanical sound. The loud rumble almost sounds like an engine of some kind.

My mind races at the possibilities. What if I'm seen? I have the appearance of being human, most heavenly beings do. Besides their massive wings, even the angels look human. But my clothes will be a dead giveaway that something's up. Judging from my recent bout of bad luck, I'm liable to end up in a mental ward with some of my more unsavory creations.

But if they keep going, it'll take so much longer for me to get out of this mess. The sound gets closer, and I know my time to debate my options is running short.

Six of one, half a dozen of another. I squirm out of my robes, having decided that I'd rather be found naked than dressed in a heavenly robe. I'm struggling to get my gold sandals off my feet before the airboat rounds the corner. Once I do, I sink the garments into the water and stand on them.

As the airboat approaches, I realize there's no way they'll hear me over all that noise. If I duck into the water, they'll go right on by. Then I'll have the freedom to make my own way out. But the temptation to reach out to the first human I've ever met in the flesh is too great. I crouch there nervously, my head just above the surface, ready to duck down if I change my mind.

But once I see them, my heart starts racing. This is it. The desire to make contact is too strong to deny. I start waving my hands, keeping most of my naked body concealed underwater. The airboat driver slows the boat dramatically, and I know I've been seen. The boat slowly ambles toward me.

"What the blazes are you doing out here?" the driver asks after cutting the engine and lowering his headset. He's a large man, with a piece of grass between his teeth and a thick southern accent. His passengers, two adults and three kids who appear to be a family, seem scared, but the father—a clean-cut man in cargo shorts and a white polo shirt—immediately gets up from his seat and lays down on the boat, reaching out for me.

I hesitate. "I've lost most of my clothing in my…" I pause. Instinctually, I feel I shouldn't tell them anything. But I'm not accustomed to lying either. It's immoral, and so not something we do in the heavens. There is no need. "In my travels."

The airboat driver just sits back and smiles, as if I'm not the first naked man he's come across in the swamp. I eye the children, seated in the back row near their mother, but the man's hand doesn't waver. "We're not leaving you here. No matter how naked you are," he says, staring at me earnestly with big, brown eyes.

"There's a blanket in the tool box, if one a y'all wants to get it," the driver says.

The woman goes to the toolbox while the man grabs my arm, and the force of the connection steals all the breath from my lungs. I *made* this man. Spun him from nothing. I see his entire life play out, and I know his purpose. He's kind, compassionate, and emotional, quick to both anger and forgiveness. I made him and his wife, a beauty with short, dark hair, huge, ghostly gray eyes, and olive skin, for each other. They're two parts of a whole, and together, they made a beautiful family. It is wonderfully jarring to see my work in the flesh.

I must've visibly startled at the man's touch, because he reaches around with his other hand. "It's okay. I've got you."

The man looks into my eyes with such compassion; I can't help but take his hand with my other arm. We work together to get me out of the muck. It takes some doing, and we rock that little airboat around quite a bit, but after a few minutes of struggling, I manage to clamber onto the boat. Within moments, I'm properly covered.

Without hesitating to ask me any questions, the driver fires up the boat, and we're off. Though I get plenty of curious glances from the family, they can't speak to me on the way back to the dock because of the noise. There wasn't an extra headset on board, but I don't mind the racket. It gives me time to come up with a story. An explanation. *Something.*

As we race back toward the dock, I feel like my brain is still stuck back in the muck. I'm not thinking fast enough. I can't concentrate on coming up with a story when the wind is in my face, and the astounding noise of the airboat is filling my ears. It's an absolute assault on my senses, which are accustomed to the ordered world of the heavens. I can't decide if I should block it out or let it wash over me.

But before I can arrive at some middle ground, we arrive at our destination. As we pull up, a few workers meet us at the dock to help tie up. I can tell from their uniforms that they're all a part of the same tour group. "I see you picked someone up, Marshal," one of them says to the airboat driver.

"This here is a gen-u-*ine* swamp man," Marshal says with a smile. I don't see what's so funny about it.

Neither does the man who helped me onto the boat. "What's so funny?" he demands.

"I find a lot of things out here in the swamp. It's not as rare as you might think to find a man out there, though it is rare to find one alive. Not even a nibble taken outta ya by a gator, a snake, or any other of God's creatures?" He shakes his head and whistles. "You got some luck."

"If getting stranded in the middle of the swamp is luck, I'm not sure I want it," I say.

The man who pulled me from the muck chuckles. "My name is Cody. And this is my wife, Aida, and our three children, Columbus, Eve, and Kareena." He puts his arm around the lovely woman, who cradles their three children between her arms. They're all staring at me with their mother's eyes.

"I'm very sorry to have cut your tour short."

"This is way cooler than any gator we might've seen in the swamp," Columbus says with a sparkle in his eyes. He seems to be between the two girls in age, maybe about eight. The older girl next to him—whom I assume is Eve—elbows him, and he yelps and rubs his arm.

I smile at them, grateful these nice people were the ones who found me.

"What happened to you? Is there anything we can do to help?" Cody asks.

"Thank you, Cody," I say, side-stepping the question. The others are all leaning in a bit, as if waiting for my answer. They're in for a disappointment. "You've already shown me such kindness. I truly appreciate it. I think I'll be all right from here."

When we clasped hands earlier, I saw how hard Cody worked for this family vacation. How many extra hours he put in before they left home, and how much he dreads going back to work because his boss is a real jerk about letting people have time off. He has a tendency to make an employee's life miserable for weeks after they come back as punishment. But Cody has missed so much time with his family that he finally put his foot down. He knows in his heart he's finally made the right type of sacrifice.

And I agree. The move will lead Cody to look for other employment. It will be hard for a while, but the new job, the one he never would've looked for otherwise, will be so much better for him and their family. I smile in excitement for them.

If I take any more of their time, I worry I might impact that delicate future.

"Oh, come on now. We can at least give you a ride into town. Maybe take you to a hospital or police station so you can report what happened?" Aida suggests.

I hesitate, and Cody pushes. "At least come back with us. I have some extra clothes you can have at the hotel. You'll need something to wear until you can get yourself back home."

The tourism workers look on, watching this act of kindness unfold in silence.

"We have to go back to the hotel anyway. Just come with us. It's not out of our way at all," Cody tries, one last time.

I look back at Marshal. "I'd take the offer, man," he drawls. "Lord knows you ain't getting nothing from the likes of me." He chuckles. I know the man isn't the most upstanding citizen, a true grey thread if there's ever been one, but at least he's honest. That's something I can respect.

"All right then. Thank you, Marshal, for stopping."

The man nods, and with that, I'm on my way to civilization.

When we get to the car, Cody offers some dirty clothes to me for the ride—a pair of pants and a shirt. I can tell he's embarrassed, and Aida is clearly mortified, but I appreciate the gesture.

"Hey, it's still cleaner than me. I just spent a few hours in the swamp." The kids laugh as they climb into the huge SUV, and I slip on the pants and shirt before piling in after them.

The hotel is a long way from the swamps, which doesn't surprise me much. After a few miles of strained silence, I laugh to myself. From the covert looks they keep turning to give me, I can tell the children are just about bursting with questions. Even though Cody and Aida have more tact, it's clear they're almost as curious. I decide to ease their minds a bit. After all they are doing for me, they deserve it.

"I never explained what happened to me, did I?" The three heads of the children whip around to the back, where I sit alone in the last row. Two of the kids still sit in booster seats, so it really takes some work for them. Aida looks curiously over her shoulder too, and Cody tips his head slightly to the right to listen while keeping his eyes on the road.

I clear my throat, searching for the right words to use. This will be difficult because I still don't want to lie. "Let's just say I fell."

"I told you he was an angel." The youngest, who looks to be around six, whispers loudly to her sister. Eve eyes me with wide-eyed suspicion, obviously starting to believe her little sister.

I smile at her. "I'm not an angel; I can tell you that for sure." Kareena frowns with disappointment. Eve keeps staring at me, as if she knows instinctually there's more to me than I'm willing to reveal, but she keeps quiet.

Columbus has much more fantastical ideas about my origins. "Are you like James Bond? Did you fall out of a flying jet while trying to disarm some enemy nuclear device?" He's talking a mile a minute. "Or maybe you jumped out of an airplane, and you landed in a secret location in the swamp in order to communicate with aliens?"

A good, long laugh claims me. "You have a wonderful imagination. Never lose that." Columbus looks at me in expectation, waiting for an answer, and I chuckle again. "No, I'm not a spy or anything fun like that. I just seem to have stumbled on hard times. Stumbled quite badly, it would seem."

Aida and Cody share a look, and I hurry to make light of my situation, so they won't feel obligated to do more than they already have. "But things are looking up. I have direction." Aida and Cody glance at each other again, having a silent conversation, and I feel there's nothing more I can say to comfort them, so I look out the window and watch the landscape change from swamp, to dense woods, to scattered homes, to urban sprawl, and then to city.

I try not to focus on how overwhelming it is to be in the car, watching the scenery fly by firsthand. It's an exhilarating rush that can't be appreciated by watching cars from above. I need to be present with this family, but my senses tug at me, demanding attention.

"And what exactly is that direction?" Cody eventually asks.

I debate telling them my true destination. Could it be a coincidence that this family of New Yorkers found me in the middle of a Florida swamp? They all eye me, waiting for my response, and I decide now's not the time to test my ability to lie. "New York." I try to picture Kismet in the city as we continue our drive on the busy Florida highways. It makes me smile to think of how happy she is.

"Daddy, that's where we live!" Columbus shouts.

"We are going home tomorrow," Eve offers.

Aida looks back at the children, and then looks at me, her gaze full of uncertainty. I can tell she wants to help me, but she doesn't want to risk her children to do it. And who can blame her? She has absolutely no reason to trust a stranger with her most precious gifts.

"Don't worry. I know my way around. I'm not in any kind of hurry anyway. I'll get there when the timing's right." Nothing more is said about it. At least, not right then.

Their hotel is in the heart of Orlando, and the children regale me with tales of their trip so far, all the theme parks they'd visited, how much Kareena loved meeting Mickey Mouse for the first time, and how Columbus puked on The Incredible Hulk roller coaster. I love hearing it. This family I've created loves their lives, and I couldn't be happier for them.

Eventually, we stop for dinner. The conversation is light and easy. I find human food delightful. It's so different from what we have in the heavens. Eating there is more of a social occasion than a necessity. We don't need to eat, but we do it anyway to be near each other. It's a social act entirely, though, and our diet doesn't much vary from the somewhat tasteless wafers that are our staple.

At the kids' insistence, I order something called a cheeseburger, fries, and a brown, bubbly drink. Its fizziness tickles my nose, and the burger is greasy and delicious. It's a completely wonderful experience, and I hope the obvious enjoyment I'm taking in the food doesn't make me appear too odd to them.

No one asks me any more about who I am, or where I'm

from, but I can tell by the way Cody and Aida look at me that they have more questions. Questions they don't want to ask in front of the children, for fear of the answers they might get.

When we arrive at the hotel, it's after dark. Their suite is large, and it features a separate room with beds for the children. Once they're all bathed, brushed, and ready, they're ushered off to bed. Eve protests, but Cody and Aida insist she needs a good night's sleep before the long days of travel ahead.

Once we're alone, Cody and Aida sit on the couch, and I sit in one of the lounge chairs across from them, each of us with a glass of wine.

"So, do you want to tell us what happened to you?" Cody ventures.

"It's not a matter of wanting to tell you. It's a matter of not being sure of the rules. And if those rules are broken, I don't want you and your family to get caught in it." That's the truth of it. I stare down at my wine, swirling it in the glass. I like that they offered a glass to me; it's a sign of welcome and companionship for these people.

I feel Aida's eyes on me. I know she's not judging me. Her expression tells me she's merely curious.

"What is your plan then? If I asked you to leave right now, where would you go?" she asks.

"Well, I..." I hesitate, knowing if I tell her the truth—that I will just go walk around, maybe sleep in an alley until morning when I can find a way to make some money to grab a bus to New York, she will scoff, and it will only make her feel more guilty for wanting such an odd stranger away from her children.

"Listen, maybe it's best if you don't know more about me. That way there's no guilt when we part ways, even if it's right this moment. You don't know me, and I don't—" I find myself unable to finish the sentence. I do know them, probably better than they know themselves. "At any rate, maybe less is more in this case. Don't worry about me. You've already been more than generous. In fact, I think I'll just finish my wine and go, if that's all right."

I look at Cody. "You've built a fine life." I know a little pride is coming through in my voice, but I can't help myself. "Keep on keeping on, my friend." I set my half-full glass on the coffee table between us and reach out my hand to Cody as he stands.

But the man only looks at it and frowns. "Sit down. Your wine isn't even gone." He and his wife share a look. "Are you a criminal?" he asks point blank.

I smile at the thought. "No." *At least not in the sense he thinks.*

"Is that only because you haven't been caught?" Cody persists.

That makes me laugh. "No."

"Have you ever killed anyone or hurt small children?" Aida asks.

This statement doesn't make me laugh or smile. I'm sad that she feels she has to ask it. But she does. How can Webber be right? How can the world need more dark threads to "make things interesting"? It needs more threads like Kismet's if you ask me. Beautiful families like this one shouldn't have to worry that their future might be entangled in a mass of black thread. "No," I finally answer, but as the word leaves my mouth, I think of the stillborn. No, I didn't kill him, but his ill fate was my fault. My frown grows even deeper at the thought.

"Fine then. You can come back to New York with us. We're leaving first thing in the morning, and I trust you won't delay us any more than the children?" Aida asks with a bit of a twinkle in her eyes.

I chuckle. "I'll do my best. It's not like I have a lot to pack up."

It's their turn to laugh. Cody nods toward the bathroom. "You know, if you want to get cleaned up, by all means, take advantage. I'll set out some *clean* clothes for you." He smiles as he emphasizes that the clothes he has to offer are clean this time around.

"Truly, I don't know how to thank you both."

They laugh again. "Don't thank us until we get to New York. You're about to embark on three days trapped in a car with three kids. Perhaps we should be apologizing to you."

Laughter fills their room, and as I make my way to the

shower, I know I landed right where I was supposed to be. But who wrote my fate? Did God have a hand in it? Is this kind family His last nod to a job well done while I was in the heavens? Or did one of my sisters take control once I fell? But how? It's hard to admit it, even to myself, but I'm happier than I ever was spinning threads, save for Kismet's. Sure, the work was rewarding, but meeting the people I've helped create, seeing the lives they've made for themselves… well, it's a magic I never could have imagined.

I stare at myself in the bathroom mirror as steam from the shower fills the room. My face is covered in dirt, and some of the swamp still resides in my curly, blond hair.

Shaking my head as I pick the dried leaves from my locks, I think, *Some banishment this is turning out to be.*

The water on my pale skin feels wondrous as it runs all over my body. Showers aren't something we have in the heavens. We just never needed them. There isn't any dirt or filth in heaven, nor do we sweat.

I marvel at the way my skin changes as the hot water beats down on it, transforming it to red. All the bottles in the shower are a total mystery, but I use them anyway, building up soap bubbles from head to toe.

By the time I'm done experimenting, everyone has gone to bed. Someone—Cody, I assume—made up the couch for me to sleep on. It isn't much, just a blanket and a pillow, probably off their bed, but the sight is almost enough to bring me to tears. It's as if by letting in one human emotion, I opened the floodgates to them all.

I've never been in a bed before. But while I'm not tired—I don't know how to be—my body aches in a way it never has before. The makeshift bed calls to me. Normally, my days follow an eminently predictable routine, and today has been anything but. Sinking down onto the couch, I pull the covers over me and find myself thinking not of my sisters, or the kind Michaela, or the Keeper, or Webber, but of Kismet. Her face fills my mind as my body relaxes, and I pass the night daydreaming of her.

SIX

In the morning, the kids are thrilled to see me still in their suite. They all had starry-eyed hopes of being entertained by my tales of adventure while we make the long drive from Florida to New York. But I know I can't tell them anything about my life back home. Then I remember all the human legends, fairy tales, and mythologies I've learned over the years from watching the humans in the tapestry. How much of myself can I give to them by using these stories as a guise?

I wait until the children start getting restless before I pull out the big guns. "You know, I can't tell you much about who I am, but I can tell you some of the legends about my family. Would you like that?" I say as we cross over the Georgia line.

The kids all turn around in unison and stare at me wide-eyed. I chuckle. "I'll take that as a yes." I debate for a moment and then look right at Columbus. "I have two sisters too. Did you know that?" The three kids shake their heads so hard that the girls' hair slaps the sides of their faces.

"I do. One of them is quiet and thoughtful. The other is a bit more brazen. Do you know what that means?" The description makes Aida chuckle.

"Like Aunt Amedia," she fills in. The three kids nod seriously.

I continue my story. "My sisters and I used to make up stories about people who lived in other places, almost like they lived on another planet. Do you guys do that?"

"Sometimes, I make up stories about my dolls," Eve offers.

"You create a whole life for them, don't you?" She nods, and I smile at her earnest expression.

"That's what we used to do. We did it so much, that some people said we were like the three Fates. Do you know that story?"

They shake their heads no, and I spy Aida watching me closely, trying to put the pieces together. That's okay, though—even if I were to tell her the truth flat out, she would never believe my story.

"The three Fates are said to create the lives of people on Earth. One is a Spinner, making the threads of life carefully from the dust of the universe." A quiet gasp spreads throughout the car. "The second is the Timekeeper. She decides how long that person will get to live. She cuts the Spinner's thread at just the right place, taking care to leave the person's life long or short, as she sees fit. The third decides how that life will end."

"How they die?" Eve says, barely above a whisper.

"Yes. How they die. Together, they are said to bring life to this world. A tapestry is woven from the threads of life, and it creates beauty and order from the chaos life can bring."

Aida smiles. "It's a wonderful thought." She turns around and looks wistfully out the car's windshield as she reaches for Cody's hand. I smile as he gives it a squeeze before releasing it. Kismet will have that kind of love, even if it isn't with me. And that makes me happy. At least I tell myself it does.

My smile must have faded with that thought because Eve asks, "What's wrong? Did the Fates die?"

I bring myself out of my daydream. "What? No. Fates are said to be immortal. So I'm sure they're still working away."

The kids think about that for a moment, and then I pose a question. "If you could create anyone in this world, who would it be? What would they be like?"

That subject keeps them busy until we stop for dinner. They

debate about creating good people and bad ones, painters and sports stars, boys and girls. It reminds me of the game I used to play with the others.

By the time we stop for the night, everyone besides me is exhausted. Aida and Cody thank me for keeping the kids distracted and happy. The hotel room they've found is not nearly as nice as the room in Orlando, but it's only one night, and it's a heck of a lot better than a swamp.

The kids crowd in one bed, Aida and Cody share the other, and I get set up on the floor. As I listen to the sound of the five other people in the small room sleeping, I can't help but marvel at how well everything is coming together for me here on Earth. I'm going to find Kismet. Is this my purpose after all? I can't help but wonder. But I can't let myself forget that she's fated for another man. A man I created for her.

I roll over, thinking of my sisters, my home, and the story I told the three kids. I miss Horatia and Galenia. We haven't been apart this long for centuries, and even though I am still fascinated by this new world, my fingers ache to create, to spin. But I have nothing. Absently, I pull at a thread in the blanket they gave me. I pull and pull until I have quite a length of it. Staring at it, I wonder what I can do with it. I don't have a needle, a loom, or even a crochet hook, but I work at it anyway, tying it here, looping it there. By morning, I have a small piece that looks something like a doily.

The youngest is the first to wake up. She pads over to me quietly and watches me tie the last loop. I worked a huge hole in my blanket, but I'm quite proud of what I made.

"That's pretty," Kareena says, admiring it.

I hold it out to her, and she takes it, handing me her doll in exchange. I hold it still for her while she puts the doily on the doll's head and ties it under her chin. It fits perfectly as a tiny hat.

"There," she says quietly, quite satisfied with herself.

"Oh, she looks beautiful." I didn't hear Aida come up behind us, but her words are genuine. "Where did you get that hat, honey?"

Kareena hugs her mother's leg and points at me.

"I don't understand," Aida said, her brow furrowed. "I didn't think you had anything."

"I didn't." I hold up my ruined blanket. "I got a little carried away last night." I feel bad about ruining it, and hope they won't have to pay for it, but now that I've created something with my hands, I feel better and more relaxed.

"Can Mommy borrow your doll, honey?" Kareena nods solemnly. Aida takes the toy and carries it over to Cody.

"Look at what Penn made in the night." She holds the doll out to Cody as he sits up in bed and switches on the light. Groaning, Eve throws the covers over her head, but Columbus is as curious as I spun him to be. He gets up to see what has interested his parents so much. His hair sticks out in every direction, and his father's shirt hangs off one of his shoulders, ending just above his knees.

The boy examines the doll and looks between the two adults as if waiting for something. "What are we looking at?" he asks.

"Penn made Cassandra that hat," Aida says.

"Oh. So?" he asks, clearly perplexed about the hubbub.

"So, it's lovely, don't you think? He made it without any help at all. Imagine what he could do with the right tools in his hands." Aida looks at me with awe in her eyes. I look away. Suddenly, I regret making the doily thing. I've drawn too much attention to myself. I should've just made my own way to New York. Turning my back on the family, I try to fix the hole in the blanket. It's coming along well when Cody lays a heavy hand on my shoulder.

"Penn, you have a skill. That is very useful. If you've fallen on hard times, this could help you find your way out."

I hold up the blanket. "I don't know about that, but at least I've used it to fix what I destroyed."

Cody examines it. "You can't even tell where the hole was. How did you manage that?"

Aida comes over to see for herself. "It was at least the size of a baseball! How *did* you manage that?"

I shrug. "Carefully."

Abruptly, Aida orders a room-service breakfast and gives

the kids a to-do list. Once they're good and busy, she and Cody go into the bathroom to "get ready."

But I know they're talking about me. I suspect they want to help me more, but I wish they wouldn't. Their fate is already planned out, and it doesn't involve me, not at all. To be fair, no one's does. The uncertainty of my impact on their life leaves me uneasy. They're too good. I don't want to be responsible for something bad happening to them because I stepped in at the wrong time.

I glance at the kids, who have huddled together on the bed to watch a cartoon now that their parents aren't watching them. Once we get to New York, I have to separate myself from them. No matter how hard it is. No matter how good it feels to be with them.

But without any forms of identification, I have no way to find a job or a place to live. I have no idea how I'm going to make do on my own.

The next two days pass by too quickly for me, though I'm sure they're much slower than the children would like. The Struhl family lives in a suburb just outside the city. Kismet was living in Manhattan when I last saw her. I will need to do some research to find out if she's still there, but it shouldn't be too much of a hike once I know how to find her.

For the rest of the drive, there's no discussion about what I will do when they get home. No pressure, no brainstorming—nothing.

It's late when we pull into the driveway of the two-story brick family home. The parents and kids all drag themselves into the house, automatically finding their respective places to sleep. Wordlessly, Cody produces blankets and pillows for the couch in the living room downstairs, which folds out into a rather comfortable bed. The rest of the family is already upstairs.

Before he leaves me alone, he says one thing. "This isn't permanent, you know." But his tone isn't unwelcoming or hostile. It's as if he's saying it to comfort me, to reassure my by letting me know they're still thinking of me, still trying to come up with a solution.

I can only nod at the man, wondering how he became such a compassionate person. Did I create that quality in him, or did Cody do that on his own after I gave him a small push in the right direction?

Being accepted into this family has impacted me in a way I never imagined possible. The longer I live on Earth, the more my banishment feels like a privilege, not a punishment.

———————————

That night, I use the family's computer—a fascinating device to use firsthand—to search for Kismet's address. She's in a few small off-Broadway plays, so she's not hard to find. There's even an online interview with her that mentions the diner where she works. The Internet is a wonderful and terrible thing.

After I fold the sheets and leave them in a neat pile on the end of the couch, topped with the pillow, I sit down to write a note thanking the Struhl family for their kindness.

But Aida comes down the stairs and into the kitchen before I'm done. "You're up early."

"So are you," I say, hoping she doesn't pick up on the mild irritation in my voice.

"What are you writing?" She glances over my shoulder to read the note, but I try to squirrel it away. Laughing, she snatches it from me. "Are you kidding me? I have three kids, and the oldest is a girl. She's always trying to hide notes from boys. You've got to be quicker than that to get one over on me." Her face falls as she reads the incomplete note.

"You're leaving, just like that?" The hurt in her voice stings, making me wince.

"I figured it was the only way you would let me go."

She frowns and casts the note down in front of me like it's trash. "You're probably right. But I caught you." She goes to the coffeemaker—which scared the living daylights out of me when it started automatically about ten minutes after I sat down. "Where were you going to go?"

"There's a diner in Manhattan I'd like to visit."

"A diner?" My answer clearly confuses her.

"A diner, yes."

"Were you planning to get a meal there?"

"Maybe, but that's not really the point."

"What *is* the point?" She holds her cup with both hands and brings it to her lips, hesitating for just a moment, allowing the steam to curl around her nose.

"Kismet." It's the first time I've said her name out loud. It fills the air and lightens the room. I can't help but smile at Aida as I say it.

"Destiny," Aida says, smiling back at me. I knew the meaning of the name Kismet's parents had picked out for her, but I'm surprised Aida has picked up on it.

"Don't look so shocked. I like to read a bit of Persian literature now and again. The name isn't as uncommon in those books. And a girl gets curious." She shrugs as she sips her coffee. "So, you're in love." I know she's smiling without even looking at her. I can hear it in her voice. "For how long?"

"Her whole life."

Aida sighs. "How romantic." She pauses. "And also a little creepy. You loved her when she was an infant? You're not that old. How old is she now?"

"It's not what you think." I scramble to come up with a plausible tale that isn't a lie, but I come up short.

A smile tugs at the corners of her eyes as she watches me struggle. She's enjoying this, I realize.

Clearing my throat, I try to go on. "She and I are not meant to be together. I just want to see her. Maybe get some closure and move on. That's all."

Only then does Aida's face fall. "What do you mean? You're not going after her? Then what's the point?" She set her coffee on the table and slouches over it, as if her disappointment weights too heavily on her for her to lift it to her mouth again. She's a hopeless romantic, just the way I made her.

"I've been making mistakes. I need to move on from her. Closure will help with that." I say it firmly, even though a tiny part of me hopes it isn't closure I'll find, but love.

No. I shake my head, not allowing myself to think that way, even for a moment. Her fated mate will have no purpose without her. If I allow myself to act on my selfish thoughts, I will be destroying his life as surely as I destroyed that of my short, brown thread.

But I can't help it. Her face flashes in my mind again, and her eyes sear me right down to my being. "I need to see her." That, I know, is the absolute truth.

"Where is this diner?"

"Manhattan."

"My brother owns a bridal shop down there. I wanted to take you today anyway. I think you would make a fine tailor, and he always has openings for good workers." She nods as if it's settled, but there are some serious problems with this plan.

"I don't have any paperwork. No driver's license, social security card, nothing. I can't work yet. Not legally."

She scoffs. "Well, you're certainly not going to freeload off us for the rest of your life." A small smile lets me know she's needling me. "My brother pays a lot of his staff under the table. He even has a few small apartments above the shop for anyone who needs somewhere to stay. I'm sure you can work something out with him. He'll be thrilled to have someone so talented on board, and you can get your paperwork sorted when you have time."

"I've never done bridal work before." It isn't an excuse, more like a statement… maybe even a question. Can I do it? I'm going to be on Earth for quite a long time, so I might as well pick up a trade. If I don't like it, nothing says I have to stay. I can earn some honest money, and besides, it will keep my hands busy.

The more I think about it, the more I like the idea. "Okay. If your brother likes me and needs the help, I'd love to try it."

Aida beams. "Good. We've already agreed that Cody will handle the kids today. It's his last day off, and he wanted to spend it with them anyway. Give me a few minutes to get dressed, and then I'll drive you to that diner."

SEVEN

My anxiety compounds based on our proximity to the diner. When I created Kismet, it was almost like a miracle. I never dreamed I'd actually get to meet her in real life. My emotions swing wildly from elation to extreme, gut-wrenching fear.

Aida reaches over and sets her hand on mine. "It'll be okay. No matter what she says."

But what am I hoping she'll say? 'Oh Penn, I love you so much, take me away with you?' No, that's ridiculous. I might know her, but we've never met. Even if she agrees to sit down and take a short break to talk to me, it's complicated. The more time we spend together, the less time she'll have to meet her true love.

"I'm not sure this is such a good idea," I say as we pull into the parking lot of the diner where Kismet works. "She might not even be working today."

"I can feel it. This is fate. She's working today," Aida says confidently. "I mean, just look at this parking spot I got. It's right across from the diner. You can't get any more serendipitous than that!"

Her enthusiasm is almost contagious. But I know it's the exact opposite of fate. Before I can stop her, she's out of the car and waiting impatiently for me by the door.

Original counters, booths, and tables adorn the sixties-style restaurant, and the floor is decorated with oversized black and white tiles. A bell rings as we walk through the door.

"Have a seat anywhere you like, honey," says a blonde waitress with curly hair.

"I'm not going to sit with you," Aida whispers into my ear. "I just wanted to make sure you actually came inside. Get a table, order some pie, and talk to her. You're not leaving here until you do. I'll be waiting in the car." Aida jams a twenty into my hand, turns, and walks out. A heavy sigh escapes me, but I'm here. I'm committed.

Gulping hard, I take a seat at the nearest booth, close enough to the door that I can make an easy escape if need be. Then she comes in, and it's as if my world stops turning. Nothing moves but her. Everything else fades away, leaving only her. She has her hair wound into a messy bun on the back of her head, pencils sticking out of it, and loose tendrils tumble around her face. She wears a white, button-up blouse, paired with a black pencil skirt covered in a plain black, utilitarian apron. The only shock of color comes in the form of the bright red pumps she confidently wears as she strides to my table.

My mouth goes dry as she approaches. "Hi. I'm Kismet, and I'll be your waitress today. Can I get you something to wet your whistle? Coffee or maybe some tea?" She clears away a few of the standing menus and puts napkins on the table, all without looking at me. Finally, she meets my eyes.

She stops for a moment, as if something about me makes her pause, but her warm smile gives me the confidence to speak.

"Would you like to join me for a piece of pie?" My voice comes out quiet and squeaky, and I clear my throat in an effort to bring it back to full capacity.

"I would love to, but I have a few hours left on my shift." It rolls off her tongue smoothly, and I know she's been propositioned many times by the men in the diner. And even a few women. She has a magnetic attraction about her, and her rather melodic voice only seals the deal.

Just then, the hostess walks by and nudges Kismet with her hip. She whispers something into her ear, and I think I see the faintest hint of blush flash across her lovely cheeks. She slaps at the hostess as she walks away.

"Sandi, cover Kismet's tables for a bit, will you?" the hostess yells.

I search for Sandi and find her behind the counter with two plates of steaming food in her hands. She glances between Kismet and me and smiles. "Sure thing." She adds a wink in Kismet's direction, at which point Kismet waves her tablet of white paper in surrender. "All right, fine."

She turns back to me. "Apparently, I'm free for a few minutes." She calls out to Sandi. "Bring us a piece of chocolate pie, will you?"

"One piece?" Sandi eyes her mischievously, but Kismet ignores the leading comment and glance as she settles into the booth across from me.

I have trouble focusing with her so close, and she chuckles at my obvious struggle. "So, why don't you tell me something about yourself? You know my name. What's yours?"

"Penn." My voice is still aloof, hiding like the coward it is.

"Penn. That's an interesting name." She chuckles, and the sound feeds my soul, lifting my spirits in an instant. "I suppose it's no more unusual than Kismet. I've never seen you in here before, Penn. What's on your mind?"

"What do you mean?" I ask, not sure I want to cut to the chase this quickly.

"Seems like you came in here with a purpose." She hooks a stray piece of hair behind her ear and peers at me from behind long, dark lashes. She isn't trying to be coy, which makes her even more desirable.

Feelings I've never imagined experiencing firsthand wash over me as I watch her watching me. The blatant desire, which was dulled when I was watching her from on high, is more acute than I can bear. How do humans even function when they're constantly bombarded by feelings like this? After clearing my throat yet again, I say, "I just wanted to meet you."

"Have we met before?" Her instincts are telling her there's more to this meeting than I'm letting on, but she can't put her finger on it. I won't let her.

"No. We haven't."

She eyes me, starting to grow suspicious. "Okay, well, you better throw me a bone here real quickly, because you're turning into a bit of a creeper."

I hesitate. Maybe it's best if it ends this way. She can go her way, and I can live out my banishment in peace, knowing she doesn't want anything to do with me.

"Okay, you're gorgeous, so I'm going to give you one more chance."

I cough on the water I'm sipping. She thinks I'm *gorgeous*.

"Seriously, what planet are you from with that curly, blond hair and perfect skin? And those eyes? It's almost not fair. But you need to kick it up a notch," She wrinkles her nose at me, but her eyes are twinkling a bit.

Sandi brings us our pie at exactly that moment, and she gives Kismet a stern look. "Don't look at me like that. He's being creepy. Tell her, Penn. You know how you're acting. Even if it's just because you're nervous."

I look at Sandi helplessly, but she only shrugs and sets two spoons down on either side of the plate. "Good luck," she says, but I'm not sure if the comment is meant for Kismet or for me.

"So, what do you do?" Kismet asks as she takes a bite of the pie. She gestures toward the lonely spoon on the other side of the plate. "Come on, help me out here. It'd be rude to watch me pig out on this. Be a gentlemen and eat your share." She takes another bite of the pie, adding through a mouthful of chocolate, "Oh, and answer my question."

"I'm on my way to interview at Feldman's Bridal downtown," I say quietly as I take my spoon and toy with the pie. I don't think I can eat. My heart is pounding, and I fear I'm visibly sweating in front of her. Why did I put myself through this torture? And yet, sitting here with her, I know there's nowhere else I'd rather be.

Her eyes take on a starry expression. "Feldman's. I'd love to shop in there someday. Just haven't met the right guy yet. And don't go thinking you fit that bill for a second."

My eyes automatically go straight to hers. "I don't."

My answer startles her, and her expression turns serious. "You don't? Then why ask me to sit down?"

"Because I wanted to meet you."

"But why? Did you see me in a play or something?"

That's it, my out. Nodding, I look down at the pie and shovel a bite into my mouth. Despite the fact that the pie is smooth and moist, and chocolate is *delicious*, my dry mouth makes it difficult to swallow. I grab my glass of water from the table and take a long drink from it, trying to wash the pie down.

Kismet leans back in the booth, watching me with a smirk on her face. "So, you're an admirer. Which play did you go see?"

"*Madame Curie: The Musical.*" I watched it in the weaving room. Although it wasn't the most high-budget play, she was brilliant in the role.

I don't look back up at her, fearing... well, I don't know. That I'll give myself away? That she'll see me for who I am? That she'll turn me away, and I'll never see her again? That she'll actually fall in love with me, and her life will be worse for it? Maybe all the above.

"Oh gosh. Not my best work. I'm not sure the sad tale of Marie Curie lends itself easily to a musical. You'll have to come see me in the one I'm working on now. It's going to be great." Then, as if she realizes her blunder, she backpedals. "I mean, I don't want to be too forward. Wow, that was arrogant. I'm just excited about this new play." Her green eyes sparkle, lighting up the tiny, golden flecks inside. "The writer is totally brilliant. It's his first musical that's actually being performed, and I'm so excited to be a part of it. It's based on one of my favorite books from when I was a kid, *The NeverEnding Story*. But it's told from the Childlike Empress's perspective, and she's not helpless like she was in the book. She's a total badass." She pauses for a minute. "I think it's going to be special."

I know she's right. After all, this was planned. The play will be a huge success. People will say that it launched her career. She will go on to do her dream roles in *Phantom of the Opera*, *Les Mis*, and *Wicked*, to name a few. She will be offered roles in huge movies, but her home is on stage, and that's where she will thrive.

As I listen to her talk so passionately about her future, I know the time has come for me to leave, to walk away forever. The path I've put her on is making her happy, and I'll only get in the way. But I can't do it. With her sitting there in front of me, a vision of heaven, I know I will never be able to walk away from her unless she asks me to leave. "I wouldn't miss it."

She beams at me, and it's all the validation I need. In that moment, I don't care if it's wrong or right. She's happy, so how could it be so wrong?

"So, what do you hope to do for Feldman's?" she asks as we get down to the last few bites of pie.

"I'm a fairly good tailor. I think that's what he has in mind for me."

"He?"

"The owner. My friend is his sister. That's how I landed the interview."

"Well, good luck then. You like to…" She pauses. "Sew?" A smirk plays across her face as she waits to see how I will respond to this challenge to my masculinity.

"Hey, it's not such a bad skill to have. And I've *never* cried after pricking my finger. That makes me pretty macho, I think." I have no idea where that came from, but she laughs out loud at my response.

As we finish up the pie, we chat more easily. A small voice in my head warns me about what I'm doing. *Stop it*, it says. *You'll only make it harder to walk away when she meets her true love.* But I don't want to listen. Not now that she's right in front of me, within my reach. But I don't touch her. I can't. I know that once I do, I'll never be able to let go.

"Well, Penn, this was a pleasant surprise. I'll hold you to your promise to see my play. It opens in two weeks." She relays all the details, and I promise to come on opening night.

She stands and gathers the plate and spoons. "This one's on the house, Penn. Thank you for stopping in today." I nod and she walks away, smiling. I don't miss the look the hostess and Sandi share as she walks past them, mischievous, self-satisfied smiles on both of their faces.

I walk back to the car in a bit of a daze. It went well. We like each other. She invited me to a play in a couple of weeks. I will see her again.

When I slide into the passenger seat of the car, Aida doesn't press me for details, at least not right away. She steals little glances at me instead, her smile growing ever wider as she watches me gaze dumbfounded out the window. Before I have time to even register everything that's happened, she's parked near the bridal shop.

The shop is small but modern. Aida says hello to the receptionist—who gives me a once-over that makes me more than a little uncomfortable—and keeps walking. I glance once over my shoulder at the receptionist, who's biting her bottom lip as I walk away. Hastily, I turn back around and follow close behind Aida, taking in the minimalist aesthetic of the shop as she leads the way through it. Only a few dresses hang here and there, with plants, mirrors, pedestals, and cherry wood columns arranged artfully around the space. I want to stop to admire the fabrics, but Aida keeps walking toward the back, so I reluctantly follow.

"Cedric," she calls out as she pushes through a door marked EMPLOYEES ONLY without hesitation.

"Back here," he calls back.

I'm overwhelmed. All different kinds of white fabric surround me. Whereas there were only a few dresses displayed in the front of the store, the back is packed to the gills with stock. To my horror, Aida disappears into the sea of fabric, leaving me slack-jawed, my back pressed against the EMPLOYEES ONLY door.

"There you are," I hear Aida say, and I try desperately to find her voice through the maze of chiffon, lace, and taffeta.

"Cedric, this is Penn, the one I was telling you about." She must have turned to look back at me, because she clucks her tongue. "Penn, where have you gone to? Come meet Cedric."

"I'm afraid I'm a bit lost," I shout back to her. She laughs and sticks an arm into the air, waving it about for me to see.

"Over this way."

I weave my way through the racks of dresses, trying to take the most direct route to her.

"Sorry," I say when I find them at last. "I'm afraid that's not a very good first impression." I hold out my hand for Cedric to shake. In that instant, I see his life—growing up with Aida, struggling to get his business up and running, making a close circle of friends here in the city, everything. He doesn't have a family of his own, though that's not to say he doesn't value family. Some people just don't get a true love. They are stronger on their own. He relishes his role as Uncle Cedric to Aida's kids, but he values returning to his quiet apartment when the day is done. I smile at the life he's made for himself. It's another life I created that hasn't been wasted.

"My first impression was already made when Aida told me about your skills," Cedric says. "My sister isn't known to exaggerate about things like that. She tells me you need a place to live. What do you think about an apprenticeship here in the shop in exchange for living upstairs? Of course, I will provide you with a small paycheck so you can buy food and stuff, but rent and utilities will be on me, okay? If you want to work here extra hours, your paycheck will increase. If not, that's fine too. No judgment here. Once you've proven yourself, we can discuss a regular salary."

"What about an interview?" I say, trying to process his words.

"Aida's word is enough for me, for now. I'm sure you'll prove your worth once you can start working. And if you're not a good fit, we'll figure something else out. Don't worry. We're not the kind of family that turns our back on someone in need."

That, I already understand. I smile, grateful I literally land-ed in this family's lap. "I'm not sure what I would have done without you," I say to Aida. She puts her arm around me and squeezes.

"Just get to work, okay? I should go rescue Cody from the kids. Keep in touch. And come for dinner on Sunday. That's not a request. Cedric can bring you." She looks sternly at her brother, who nods and holds up his hands in surrender.

"We'll be there," he says. She hugs her brother goodbye, and I watch her leave, not sure how I feel about seeing her go. She became important to me in the short time we've known each other. I don't relish the idea of being apart from her, but I'm not even supposed to be part of her life. I'm a Fate, and for all I know, my actions here will have a ripple effect. One that will now affect Cedric.

Once Aida's gone, her brother turns to face me. He doesn't look much like her. Where Aida's hair is dark brown, his is black, parted down the center, falling just below his ears; where her face is long and slender, his is more round; and they are totally different heights. But they share the same gray, almond-shaped eyes.

His navy suit is tailored to fit him almost perfectly, but I spot a few places where it could be better. I'm not sure how I know this, having not spent much time around either humans or their clothing, but it just looks off to me.

Cedric sees me looking at his suit and pulls on one sleeve. "Do you like this suit? I had it made for me by a new guy down the street. I like to support local businesses, but I'm not convinced. It's nice, but a little overpriced if you ask me."

I hold out my hand. "Do you mind?"

It takes a moment for Cedric to understand what I want, but he eventually takes off his jacket and hands it to me. But once I have it, I'm not sure how to make the changes it needs. I scan the room for a needle, thread, scissors, and other basics.

"What are you looking for?" Cedric asks.

"Needle and thread."

"I don't…" He hesitates, but then changes his mind. "You know what, let's see what you can do. Right this way."

He leads me over to my new workstation, complete with a

sewing machine, an array of needles, thread spools, pins, fabric swatches, tape measurers, scissors, seam rippers, and other odds and ends I will need. Glancing at again the length of Cedric's arm, I get to work.

"Aren't you going to measure?" he asks, but I don't answer.

"This might take me a few minutes, if you have something else you'd like to do," I suggest, but he stands still, apparently entranced by the movements of my hands.

It takes me more than a few minutes; in fact, it takes a few hours. After a while, Cedric pulls up a chair and sits beside me, completely mesmerized. I fumble a little, not fully understanding the unfamiliar fabric, but once I get used to the tools and the materials, I see the solution and work toward it.

"I think that should do it," I finally say, holding up the coat for Cedric.

Giving me a skeptical look, Cedric puts one arm into the jacket, and then the other. I smooth the shoulders and back, knowing that the fit is now perfect.

We walk to the closest full-length mirror, and Cedric takes in the effect of my work. "Sorry that took me so long," I say. "Sewing isn't really my forte. Spinning is."

"Spinning?" Cedric asks without looking at me. He is too busy admiring himself in the mirror.

"I think you would call it fabric making? Weaving? Creating." I can't hide the smile on my face as I think of how much I enjoyed making that silly little hat for Kareena's doll.

"Spinning, huh?" He turns a bit and looks over his shoulder at his back in the mirror. "I don't know. You're pretty good at tailoring, if you ask me. In fact, I'm not sure how much I can teach you. I didn't even realize this wasn't a good fit." He says it under his breath, almost to himself, and I smile, pleased to have made this man happy.

He clears his throat and glances down at his watch. "All right, well, it's nearly closing time. Tell you what. Take what you need and spin something for me tonight. Play around. Your apartment is upstairs, fully furnished and ready for you. Here's the key." He hands me a small key ring with an "I Heart NY" keychain on it. "If you need anything at all, I'm sure one of your neighbors will be happy to help. I didn't intend to spend my entire afternoon with you, so now I need to play some catch up." He steals a glance at his reflection one more time, taking in the craftsmanship of the coat.

"Highly overpriced, that man," he says as he turns and leaves.

Looking around the shop, I revel in the fact that he's given me the freedom to spin anything I want. Not a specific person, not a specific garment. Anything. But, being that I'm in a bridal shop, I figure a dress might be most useful for Cedric.

I'm not sure I can prepare an entire dress in one night, especially considering I've never made anything larger than a doily slash hat. But I hope having the right materials on hand will ensure my success. Happy to have a purpose for the night ahead instead of lying around pretending to sleep, I settle in to my workstation, letting the movement of my hands take me away.

I don't notice the others coming and going. Occasionally, someone stops to watch me for a bit, but they never speak. Somehow, they know not to interrupt me. I'm in a zone of creation, and I don't pour less of myself into my work just because I'm making a dress, not a person.

I never make it up to my apartment that night. Instead, I spend the twilight hours bent over my work, crafting the lace, adding beads, and sewing it together to make the most beautiful dress I've ever seen. I picture Kismet wearing it as she walks down the aisle toward... her true love. Not me, but her true love. I shake my head as I make some adjustments. The lace bodice has capped sleeves, and there are scalloped edges along the bottom of the gown. The patterns in the lace create the appearance of galaxies similar to those I spent my life admiring from my bedroom window in the heavens. Swirls of fabric and beads create a beautiful universe contained in a single dress. I arrange the piece on a dress form and walk around it, pausing now and again to add some finishing touches.

A few people start to arrive for the day, and they stop and gasp as soon as they see the dress. "Were you here all night?" someone asks, but so many people have gathered around my masterpiece that I can't tell who spoke.

"What's the hold up here?" Cedric shouts from the back of the group. "I'm trying to get through."

When he sees the dress hanging on one of their older mannequins, his breath catches. "Where did this come from?"

I can't read his tone. Is he upset? I'm crouched around behind the form, fixing the hem on the back of the dress, when Cedric approaches, and I debate staying there to assess his reaction. But I stand slowly instead, deciding to be brave.

Cedric stares at me in disbelief, then his eyes naturally return to the dress. "How is this possible? You said you weren't good at sewing. Where did this fabric even come from?"

Someone in the back clears his throat. "We don't carry this fabric."

I start looking for the source of the voice, but my search is cut short by Cedric. "So, did you get it somewhere else on short notice, Penn? How could you have created something like this in a little over twelve hours?"

I feel somewhat sheepish, like I've done something wrong. The longer I'm on Earth, the more I'm discovering that I don't face the same limitations humans do. Making the dress in a single night wasn't much of a stretch for me. In fact, I feel energized by it.

"I made the fabric, sir. I told you I was better at spinning than sewing."

"But this…" He trails off as he circles the dress. "It's a work of art." He folds his arms over his chest for a moment, and then says, "What do you plan to do with this dress, Penn?"

"You asked me to spin something for you, so I did." I think of Kismet wearing it, but then I make myself say, "I made it with your materials. You do with it as you see fit."

Cedric smiles. "The possibilities…" He trails off again, and I can see his mind working as his eyes dart back and forth over the dress. "Penn, I'm going to set up a team meeting this afternoon to see how much of our resources we can devote to you. And if this is indicative of the kind of work you do, I'll increase your salary substantially. You're no apprentice, my friend. You're a master. This is going to be big. Thank you."

I can't believe my ears. "No, thank *you*. This opportunity means a lot to me. I don't want to let you down. Ever." I think again of my mistake with the short, brown thread. But it won't be possible for me to mess up like that here. There just isn't as much riding on bridal fashion.

Cedric claps me on the back and shakes my hand. "This is going to be a beautiful friendship, I think."

He smiles as he walks away, and for a moment, I'm feeling pretty good about my future on Earth. Then I spot someone lingering behind.

The bottom falls out of my stomach as he approaches. I recognize him immediately. He has dark, straight hair cropped short on the sides and combed over, thick, black eyebrows accentuating dark eyes, and a lean but strong build. Even though I didn't get a clear picture of him on that fateful day, I know in the depths of my broken soul that this is Kismet's true love.

EIGHT

He approaches casually, his dark eyes full of curiosity and excitement. He's plenty attractive in a boy-next-door kind of way, but I know he isn't a player. He's loyal—a quality that makes him even more appealing to women.

At first, I bristle. I don't want to know him. I want to stay as far away from him as possible. But I inserted myself into their lives. Since I went out of my way to meet Kismet, it makes sense that I have put myself in his path too.

As I battle internally with myself, he gazes at the dress, temporarily forgotten by me.

"It really is lovely. Well done…" He trails off as he holds his hand out for me to shake, hoping I will fill in my name.

I stick out my hand, trying to hide my disappointment and irritation. "Penn." In an instant, I see his whole life up until that point. I take a deep breath, trying to bring myself back to what he's saying, but I'm distracted. He's had tragedy in his life, and it hurts me. Recent tragedy. His parents died in a car accident less than a decade ago. He was in college.

"Andrew," he says. I try to push down the pain I feel for his loss and focus on the present moment. He doesn't seem to be hurting too much anymore, at least not actively, so I shouldn't either. "I work in accounting," he adds. "It's going to be my job to see how much money we can get to you for things like materials and marketing. I've seen that look on Cedric's face before. He's going to want to push you, just to see how far you can go."

I really want to dislike Andrew, but dang it, he's friendly. *Of course* he's friendly. I made him that way. I didn't want some jerk fawning after Kismet. No, her true love has to be just as charming and full of light as she is.

"I don't really know what to say to that," I say. And that's the truth. It's all a lot to take in. Becoming a golden boy again after falling so far—literally—is a bit much for me to absorb at the moment.

Andrew smiles, and the expression lights up his face, making me want to see it again. A small part of me hates him for it. Kismet will love him immediately. I know it.

A dark thought creeps into my mind as I stand there with Andrew. If Kismet never meets Andrew, she'll never fall in love with him. She can still be mine.

The disgust that boils up in my stomach leaves a horrible taste in the back of my mouth. I've never had such an actively destructive thought before in my life. Not only would I be interfering directly with Kismet's fate, but I would be stealing Andrew's real purpose. I spun him to complement her in every way. Preventing them from meeting is against everything I represent. And yet, the thought still lurks in my mind.

"Well, nice work, Penn. Very nice work. I look forward to seeing you this afternoon," Andrew says as he sticks out his hand for me to shake again.

I watch him go, and for the first time since my banishment, I wonder if my punishment wasn't harsh enough.

The afternoon is a whirlwind of meetings, numbers, suppliers, and catalogues, all tailored to me. I'm not interested in any of it. All I want to do is create. Well, that and be with Kismet. By the end of the day, I'm cranky, and Cedric can tell.

In our last meeting, he announces, "I'm going to take all of you to dinner tonight, to say thank you and to celebrate this exciting prospect. How does that sound?" Cedric puts his arm around me as he says it, and everyone cheers. A few of my new coworkers get out their phones to send texts to their loved ones, but most just seem excited.

As, well, *fate* would have it, Andrew sits himself next to me at dinner. Most of our coworkers are women—who've taken to looking at me like I'm a piece of meat—and I assume he's looking for some camaraderie. I wish he would just stay away. It's easier to hate him that way. But I'm a Fate, a heavenly being. Despite my disagreements with Webber, I'm not built for hate. And Andrew isn't a soul who's easily hated.

At dinner, we chat, laugh, and basically hit it off. I can't help but be happy to have made a real friend.

Andrew invites me to all sorts of things in the days that follow—bars, Frisbee tournaments, the movies, and over to his house to watch various sporting events on TV.

Before I know it, nearly two weeks have passed. I've had dinner with Aida and her family twice. Cedric is helping me get my paperwork pushed through the system, although I'm not sure all of it is on the up and up. Then again, without a birth certificate or any other form of identification, I don't know how we would accomplish it legally. At least this way, I'll have what I need to make a life here on Earth. I'll be here for quite some time, after all.

Things at work are going great. I made five more dresses for the shop, and each sold almost immediately. Cedric claims the shop's the most profitable it's ever been.

The only dress we don't sell is Kismet's, though that's not for a lack of customers. After stewing over it for a day or two, I asked Cedric to keep it for display, as an example of what I can do. The truth is, I'm determined never to duplicate it. I can't bear to think about anyone other than Kismet wearing it, although I don't share that detail with Cedric. Thankfully, he agrees without question, and I frequently pause to look at the masterpiece and think of Kismet.

Her play is two days away, and I'm still warring with myself about keeping Andrew away from her. So what if I don't invite him to this play? There will be others. Or so I tell myself. I don't know for sure when they're supposed to meet, but it's probably not at this play. Andrew isn't even into plays.

Deep down, in a place I want to ignore, I know the first step off track is always the hardest. After that, it gets easier and easier to sacrifice the right course of action for what feels good in the moment. Anyway, if I don't invite him to the play, what kind of friend would I be, after everything he has done to make me feel welcome in this new city? When they hit it off as they're intended to do, shouldn't I be happy for them?

Andrew stops by my workstation as I'm considering my options. "Hey, I'm just heading out to get some lunch. Do you want something?"

"Yeah, I'll go with you," I say, still not sure what to do. I know what I should do, but can I cast aside my own desires to do what's right? I've never wanted anything this much before.

Andrew chats about a TV show we both like as we walk, but I'm not really listening. Television is fascinating to me. It's almost like watching a thread in the weaving room, so it has a nice familiarity to it, plus the plotlines are amazing. No one's life is that dramatic all the time.

Finally, Andrew stops talking. "Something up, Penn? You seem a bit distracted."

I watch our reflections in the shop windows as we continue walk. We can't be more opposite. Although we're almost identical in height, I'm the light to Andrew's dark. Light isn't what Kismet needs. I made Andrew to fulfill her needs in every way. I'm just not built for that, and wishing it were otherwise won't make it so.

"Andrew, there's a play I'm going to on Friday night. I think you should go with me." I keep my eyes on my feet as we walk, not wanting to look at him.

"I'm not super into plays, Penn. But thanks?" Andrew says. His tone tells me that he realizes something else is going on here. As he tries to puzzle it out, something seems to occur to him.

"Are you asking me out?"

I stop walking and consider my options. Despite my inner turmoil, I can't pass up the opportunity to tease my new friend. It's too good. "So what if I am?" I say seriously, looking straight into Andrew's eyes with as much sincerity as I can muster.

"Oh jeez, man, I'm sorry, but you've gotten the wrong impression," Andrew sputters. "I'm not, I mean, I have no problem with it, if you are, but I just…" He trails off, jamming his hands into his pockets and looking at his feet. "Listen, I was just trying to be friendly. All the people in the shop are mostly women, so when Cedric hired another guy, I was excited to have a new friend. That's all. I'm sorry if I gave you the wrong idea." The more he says, the faster he talks, until soon, there aren't any words left.

"Well, this is awkward," I say, not quite ready to let him off the hook.

Andrew shrugs and looks a way, then gives me a half smile, attempting to reassure me that we're still okay. He starts to reach up to touch me on the shoulder, but thinks better of it and lets his arm fall back to his side.

I watch it all unfold, barely able to contain myself. Finally, I can't take it any more—my friend's attempt to comfort me in spite of his own discomfort pushes me over the edge. I burst out laughing, thoroughly startling Andrew.

"What?" Andrew asks. At first, he's genuinely confused, but I know he's caught on when he smacks me on the arm. "You played me?" I can tell he isn't really mad. I can hear the laugh in his voice, just barely held back.

"You should've seen the look on your face," I say through my tears. It feels good. It's been a while since I've laughed this hard. Maybe I've never laughed this hard at all.

The crowd on the busy downtown sidewalk maneuvers around us, some people smiling at our joy, others annoyed by the commotion.

Eventually, we compose ourselves and continue on to our destination, but before we get to the deli, I realize something—Andrew didn't accept my invitation. My friend deserves to be happy.

"Hey, so how about the play? You in? I mean, now that you know I'm not propositioning you," I persist as we turn off the sidewalk and into the deli.

Andrew gives me a sideways look. "Why? What's so great about it?" he asks, still skeptical.

"The lead."

A lightbulb comes on for Andrew. "This is about a girl! Wait, a girl for you or a girl for me?"

I take a breath. Here is my defining moment. *A girl for you.* Once it's out, I can't take it back. I hold it on the edge of my tongue for as long as possible. Placing my order at the deli counter, I go about collecting napkins, a straw, condiments, and my drink.

Once we both have our bags in hand, and we're on our way out, Andrew poses the question again. "A girl for you, or a girl for me?"

I look at him sadly. "A girl for you. A girl for you." I say it twice, as if to convince myself of the truth of that statement. I wasn't expecting to have to let her go already, and the finality of it hits me hard. To make it worse, Andrew starts asking questions about her.

"What's she like? You know I don't date much. And I wouldn't have expected you, of all people, to fix me up with someone. That's something my sister would do."

"I know. But this one is different."

"Different than what? You haven't met any of my exes. You have no frame of reference," Andrew points out.

I sigh, wondering why I should have to defend her to him. I shouldn't have to explain how wonderful she is, especially not to her true love. "Tell you what. Let's just go to the play. If you don't think she's for you, we won't stop and say hi to her at the end. We'll just go home, and I'll make up some excuse about why I didn't see her after the show. No big deal."

"So you're friends with this girl? I've never heard you talk about her before."

"You're awfully suspicious. No wonder I don't do nice things for you more often," I say with a sidelong grin.

"I don't like being fixed up," Andrew insists.

"That was in no way unclear. But this doesn't even count as a date. She doesn't know I'm bringing you, so no harm, no foul if you don't fall in love with her when you see her up on stage."

Andrew laughs out loud at that. "Penn. You've been spending too much time in the shop. People don't fall in love at first sight, at least not real love."

"Want to make a bet?" I say, suddenly feeling lucky.

We've reached the bridal shop, and Andrew smiles with undeserved confidence as he holds the door open for me. "Absolutely."

Once we settle in the back room and take our lunches out, I set the terms of our gamble. "Fine. Loser buys lunch for a month."

"A month?" Andrew says, a bit incredulous at the stakes.

"What's the big deal? You won't lose, will you? People don't fall in love at first sight. Remember?"

"Fine. A month. And I get to pick where we go."

I stick out my hand, and Andrew takes it. But before we shake, I clarify one detail. "And the *winner* picks the place to eat."

"Sounds good," Andrew says as we shake hands.

I can't help but feel like I'll win the bet, but lose the prize.

NINE

I arrive at the off-Broadway playhouse twenty minutes early, and start pacing outside as I wait for Andrew. Despite the cooler evening temperatures, I'm already sweating in my brand-new suit coat and jeans.

I've made enough extra money from my creations for the shop to buy myself an entire wardrobe. In my early days at the shop, I had to borrow all my things from Cedric, so it's nice to have my own clothes. Even Andrew gave me some basic pieces to help round out my wardrobe. The thought comes as a bit of a relief. Andrew *is* worthy of Kismet, in every way. I've done the right thing by asking him here.

Still, when I finally spot Andrew approaching, I feel a mix of relief and dread. I wasn't sure he would come. Part of me hoped he wouldn't, and the cosmos would allow me to have Kismet all for myself.

Relief wins out. As I watch Andrew walk up, dressed almost exactly as I am, I smile in spite of myself. They will be perfect together, truly beautiful. They will exude happiness in every possible way, and people will look at them and smile. Who am I to deprive the world of that joy?

We take our seats a few rows back from the front, right in the center. We have an excellent view of the stage, and despite the sense of loss I feel, I'm also excited. I've never witnessed the moment when two people I've created for each other finally meet. I know it will be special, but I have no concept of just how much.

As the lights go down, Andrew leans over. "She's the lead? Kismet?" He pronounces her name slowly, clearly unsure of how to say it. "What kind of name is that?" he whispers.

I roll my eyes. "It means destiny, you idiot. Watch the play."

The curtain rises, revealing Kismet standing on center stage. She's dressed in a flowing, white gown, with the telltale pearl dangling from the center of her forehead. She's older than the Childlike Empress from the original story, but other than that, the role suits her. The writer has changed the character slightly, so that her name comes more from her interests than her appearance.

"Nothing is… well, nothing. It's dangerous in its nothingness. Empty and all consuming," she says, holding the audience captive from her very first line.

I reluctantly tear my eyes away from her and look to Andrew, whose mouth is hanging open in disbelief as he watches her. He isn't blinking. I can tell that Kismet is speaking right to his heart. It truly is a special magic to see him react to her, his soul mate.

After the show, Andrew and I don't speak. I can tell the man isn't capable of words. I debate whether it's the right time for them to meet, but I decide it might be fun to watch Andrew stumble a bit.

So, we hang around out front for a while. Several minutes pass, and I start to wonder if she went out a back entrance. Andrew's not as impatient as I am; he's staring dreamily into the night sky.

Then Kismet appears through the door, and our breath catches at the same time. Dressed casually, she still looks every bit as magical and unearthly as she did as the Childlike Empress.

She doesn't notice us at first; she simply slings her purse over her shoulder and looks both ways, ready to face her journey home. But I interrupt that train of thought.

"Hi," I call out to her. She searches for the source of the voice, and then gives me a big smile when she recognizes me.

"You came," she says as she walks over to me. Andrew stands up and smiles handsomely at her, but she doesn't see him at first. She comes right to me and hugs me, making Andrew a bit unsure.

I relish the hug, probably lingering a bit longer than I should, but I know it will be our one and only interaction that dances with possibility this way. As soon as she sees Andrew, I will be nothing more than a friend. Anyway, Andrew will share a lifetime with her, so I can't feel too guilty about stealing an extra moment or two from my friend.

Kismet lets go and pulls back, beaming. "What did you think?"

"I thought it was amazing. Brilliant. You were perfect," Andrew says, not able to contain himself any more.

I watch as Kismet's expression goes from confused to completely enchanted. Their two souls have found each other, and it is absolute magic. The power of it takes my breath away. I can hardly believe I almost tried to keep them away from each other.

I clear my throat. "Kismet, this is Andrew. I brought him along because I thought he might enjoy your play. Seems I was right."

"Andrew, it's very nice to meet you," she says as she holds out her hand, never once taking here eyes off him. "Have you boys eaten? I'm famished after that performance."

We shake our heads no, and off we go, Kismet looping her arm through Andrew's as they walk, natural as could be, me trailing a few paces behind them. I listen as they chat easily, telling each other about their lives, careers, how they know me, dumb things about their childhoods, everything. I barely get a word in, but I'm content to sit back and watch this beautiful connection I've created. As much as I love Kismet, I'm thrilled to watch her with her true love. It tells me that these two really were my best creations.

———————————

Andrew buys me lunch every day after the play. Most days, he asks what I want, and he always treats without a word. He doesn't even object the day I suggest the new hippie vegan place down the block. The food is disgusting, but it's totally worth it to see him try to gag it down without grimacing. This daily unspoken confirmation of his feelings never fails to bring a smile to my face.

The next months are a whirlwind. Word about the miracle designer at Feldman's spreads quickly, and orders are coming in fast for custom dresses. I set up a system where I meet with a client, get to know her a little, and then create something to suit her specific personality. Some girls like more of a boho chic look; others like a lot of poof and frills; still others like a clean, sophisticated look. Each of the dresses I make is absolutely perfect for the bride for whom it's intended, tailored to her in every way.

I never let anyone else work on the dresses. A while back, Cedric offered to have the alterations department do the small work, the hemming and taking in, but I refused. The devil truly is in the details. Cedric hasn't brought it up again.

On the other side of my life, Andrew and Kismet are inseparable outside of work. They spend every available moment together, and when they're apart, they can't stop talking about each other. They often include me in their outings, but I know they also spend plenty of time alone together.

A couple of months later, I'm working on a special order for a bride when the receptionist buzzes me on the speakerphone on my table. "Penn, there's someone to see you," she says. Lowering her voice, she adds, "And you never answered my lunch invitation."

I sigh, growing tired of the constant come-ons from the women in the shop. "I'm sorry. I didn't realize I had an appointment. I'll be right up." I hate when I lose track of time and forget things, but sometimes, I get so wrapped up in the work, I lose sight of everything around me.

Before the receptionist can respond, I shrug on my suit coat and head to the sales floor, smoothing my pants as I go.

Just as I'm shaking the wrinkles out of the coat and round the corner to the front of the shop, I look up and see Kismet standing at the desk, talking animatedly with the girl behind it. I've been expecting to see her—after all, I helped Andrew shop for the ring—but it still catches me off-guard.

Kismet is starting to earn some local fame from her performance in the play, and it's clear the girl behind the desk recognizes her. Her face is on a large poster just around the corner from the shop. Clearly, the receptionist is a little starstruck, but Kismet either genuinely doesn't notice or pretends not to.

When I walk up, they're deep into the details of the latest episode of some show I've never heard of.

"Wait! Don't tell me! I have it on my DVR," Kismet says as she closes her eyes and waves her hand at the girl.

"Kismet, what a pleasant surprise," I say.

We share a warm hug that gives me strength for what I know is coming. I play dumb, so she can have the satisfaction of showing off her ring.

After our embrace, she brings her hand around and sticks it under my nose. It's a beautiful black diamond set in rose gold with tiny black diamonds swirling around the band. It fits perfectly on her hand, just like I knew it would.

"Oh Kismet, it's beautiful. Absolutely stunning. Congratulations," I say as I look into her eyes, seeing the excitement dancing in them. In fact, she's having trouble holding still. She bounces on her heels until I finally let go of her hand, and then she leaps into my arms, squealing as she goes.

I know people are looking at us, but I don't care. Her joy is contagious, and I see the smiles on their faces as I spin her around.

"Well, let's see about a dress, shall we?" I take her hand and lead her to the back room. Normally, I meet with clients in a meeting room. Over a two-hour or so meeting, I'll sketch out what they want, or what I *think* they want, then make changes and take notes. Usually, the client goes to get measured, and I go to my workstation to get started. But Kismet is special. Her dress is already done. The only problem is that Andrew has seen it.

As we walk, I ask her a few questions about the engagement. "Did you tell your parents?"

"Yes. We called them last night. But I wanted to wait to tell you. I mean, I know you already knew, but still." She shrugs. "I wanted to tell you in person. You made this happen. This smile on my face." She points to her face, making me smile with her.

"Do you want me to call Andrew down?"

"No!" she says adamantly. "He has strict instructions to stay in his office."

I nod, surrendering to the wishes of the bride, and can't help but laugh. "I want to show you something," I say as we walk past my workstation, moving deeper into the back, where I keep a lot of my materials. When Cedric requested something new and fresh for the front window, I moved her dress out of the way. Cedric, of course, asked if he could sell the dress, but I refused. I told him the dress was my muse, and I could only bear to part with it for the right bride.

And here she is.

I move a few piles of threads and fabric out of the way, and then pull the mannequin out for her.

"That's..." She trails off, holding her hand on her chest as she gazes at the dress.

"Please, take a look at the whole thing," I suggest, gesturing for her to take a lap around the entire dress.

She automatically does as she's told without making a verbal response, her mouth hanging open. She toys with her necklace to keep her hand busy as she walks around the dress. "This is perfect. Did you make it?" she asks.

"I did, my first day here. There's just one problem..." I hesitate, not sure how she will take the news.

"Did someone else buy it? Why would you show it to me if it already belongs to someone else?" The panic in her voice makes it raise at least two octaves by the end of her question, and I hold my hands out in surrender, trying to calm her down.

"No. This dress is yours if you want it."

"So what's the problem?" she demands.

"Andrew has seen it."

Her breath hitches, but a crooked smile steals across her face. "What did he think?"

"He loved it. Thought it was great work," I answer honestly. "It was months ago, so I don't remember his exact words, but he did like it."

"He'll like it even better on me," she says, walking closer to the dress and gingerly touching the beadwork on one shoulder. "I want to try it on now. Can I?"

"Of course. Meet me out front. Have one of the girls get you a room, okay? Let them know if you want champagne or anything. I'll be right up after I get the dress off the mannequin," I say.

She claps her hands and skips happily out of the back room. As I carefully remove the dress, I can't help but feel this moment is a little bittersweet. Like I have an eternity on this Earth, and my journey is already coming full circle.

Of course, the dress fits her perfectly. "It's like it was made for me," she says, the disbelief plain in her voice.

"It was," I say. "I made it the day we met."

Kismet looks at me with such love and sorrow, and her beautiful green eyes fill with tears as she reaches for my hand. Standing there on the pedestal, wearing the lace dress I made for her, she's a vision to behold. The tears spill over and run down her cheeks.

"Why are you crying?" I ask, suddenly concerned.

"Because you are so good to me. I know you love me, Penn, and I love you too, but Andrew…"

I smile in spite of myself and wipe a tear from her cheek. "I know. I know in a way that even you don't. You were quite literally made for each other."

She nods emphatically. "I love you even more for understanding. I can tell you're not just saying that to placate me. You *know*. And you still love us both."

"Of course I do." I squeeze her hand. "Now dry your tears so we can Skype your mom, okay?"

She wants to pay for the dress, of course, but I made it for her, and it's mine to do with as I please. I offer to give Cedric money for the materials, but he refuses me. He seems almost as sad as I am to see the dress go, albeit for different reasons. He calls it a work of art—the catalyst that started the shop's climb to bridal boutique fame.

Everyone has trouble being productive after Kismet walks out with the dress that day. The shop feels somehow emptier without it. But like everything else when it comes to Kismet, I know I have to set it free.

———

The following months pass by like a strong spring wind. I feel completely engulfed by their wedding plans. Andrew names me his best man, and Kismet leans heavily on me for help with figuring out most of the details. Her parents both live in Florida, and her girlfriends are proving less than helpful. But I'm happy to be included.

They often invite me over to their new apartment for dinner. It's a small studio, but it's not the indoor space they're paying for. The balcony has views of the city I could watch forever.

One night, while Kismet is washing dishes, Andrew and I sit out on the balcony watching the world go by on the street below.

"Penn, can I ask you something?" Andrew asks, his dark eyes thoughtful.

"I'm quite confident you can. Particularly based on the stunning skill with which that last question was executed."

He ignores me and goes on. "Where are you from? Why don't you ever talk about what your life was like before moving here?"

"I do. I told you about my sisters," I say carefully.

"What happened to them?"

"They're still at home, where they belong."

"Where is home?"

I don't answer him. We've danced around these questions before. Andrew hasn't persisted until now, and I prefer it that way.

"Or maybe the better question is, why aren't you comfortable telling us?" Andrew studies me, but I look out over the street, admiring the beauty I see before me.

"I would love to share that part of myself with you," I say after a moment. "But there are a lot of reasons why I can't. Anyway, you'd probably think I was crazy if you knew the truth." I chuckle, trying to shake Andrew out of his inquisitive mood, but his sidelong glance tells me it isn't working tonight. I swirl the wine in my glass and sigh.

"Would it change what you think of me? Truly? Besides, what are you thinking? That I have some big, dark past as a drug addict, murderer, or child molester? That I used to be a priest? A hippie? A battered soldier? Does it really matter what my life was like before I met Aida and her family?"

Andrew thinks for a moment. "I mean, some of those things are pretty intense. Got to say, I wouldn't want you being around my kids if you were a few of those things."

I nod seriously. "Rightfully so." My expression gives Andrew pause, and I laugh. "Wow. Good to know I can shake your opinion of me so easily."

Andrew smacks me, and we're quiet for a few moments.

"No. I guess it doesn't matter," he finally says.

I glance over my shoulder. Kismet has her back to us as she washes dishes in the sink. I can just barely hear her singing a tune from the latest musical she's headlining. Her next job will be on Broadway. As I sit next to her match, I know that both of their dreams are coming true, and the thought fills me with a feeling of satisfaction.

"You're a good man, Andrew." I hold my glass out to my friend, and we drink a toast to them, their lives, and their future.

But as I do, something nags at the back of my mind. Something I haven't thought of in a long time. I don't know if it's Andrew's questions, or if I'm just mentally comparing the friends I've made here with the ones I had in the heavens, but Michaela's pained expression flashes through my mind again as I swallow the wine. I wonder if she's resolved her problem, whatever it was. Something in the pit of my stomach tells me no, but I ignore it. After all, she's out of my reach.

TEN

Two weeks before the wedding, the world turns to ash around me. Everything I thought to be true about heaven and Earth is turned upside down in an instant.

———————

Andrew didn't come to work that morning, but I didn't even realize it until lunch came and went. Despite the fact that our month-long agreement elapsed quite some time ago, Andrew has continued to buy me lunch every day. When I said something about it a few months ago, he just shrugged and mumbled something about how he owes his happiness to me.

I start asking around about Andrew once I realize he isn't there, but no one has seen him. In fact, Cedric hasn't even heard from him, which is very unusual.

The truth becomes clear the moment Kismet walks into the store. Death can be the only explanation for the complete and utter anguish etched deep into her face.

———————

I have never known grief. I have no concept of it. Nor do I know how to handle it. So after Kismet confirms the ugly truth—he's gone forever—I hold on to her right there in the storefront, both of us sobbing, until Cedric comes out and ushers us into the back. He also calls Kismet's parents and arranges for them to come to New York on the next available flight. But I'm not paying attention to all that. Kismet is the only being in my world right now. That, and a huge, empty hole my friend once occupied.

I don't understand. How could this have happened? I saw Andrew's thread, and it was long enough to match Kismet's.

"This isn't right," I keep saying to anyone who will listen. They all think I'm just grieving the loss of my best friend.

"No, it isn't right. He was too young," they say. "So much potential, wasted." Or "It's such a shame." They don't understand. Not like I do. Something has gone terribly wrong, and I have to find out what.

Eventually, when the sobbing subsides, I learn that Andrew died in his sleep. The doctors find no preliminary signs of foul play, and it certainly wasn't an overdose. For the time being, he appears to have somehow died of natural causes… at twenty-eight. Kismet discovered him when she went home for lunch. Before leaving for her early shift at the diner, she kissed him, and he smiled and mumbled *I love you*. He was alive. He was fine. A few hours later, he was gone.

"I don't understand," she keeps saying over and over. It becomes her mantra, almost like it's what reminds her to breathe in and out. If she speaks the words, expelling air, she's forced to take more back in. It keeps her alive.

Turns out, Cedric isn't able to get her parents out until the next day, so Kismet stays at my apartment that night. She can't bring herself to return to their empty home, or sleep in the bed where he breathed his last. I don't relish the idea of being alone, either. So I let her have my bed, and I settle down to sleep on the couch in the living room.

What happened to Andrew? I remember the creation of his thread so vividly, including the relief I felt when Horatia cut it so long and Galenia decided he would die peacefully in his bed with his family around him. That didn't mean he'd slip away mid-morning in his late twenties.

What if the same thing happens to Kismet? I sit up in a cold sweat, my heart pounding right out of my chest. I can't let that happen. Moving as silently as possible, I get up and pad to my room to check on her. She's buried under a mound of covers. Her mop of hair sticks out of the top, splayed over both of my pillows. I can't see her face, but I hope she's sleeping.

Bringing my pillow and a blanket into the room, I make a nest by her bedside. Her hand dangles from the bed, and I reach for it as I settle in beside her. I will never let anything bad happen to her. That just isn't her fate.

The following day, Cedric picks up Kismet's family from the airport and takes them to their apartment. Andrew doesn't have much family left, and his few remaining relatives live locally. He was an only child, so the car accident that stole his parents left him with few surviving family members.

Kismet's parents have only met Andrew once. They flew to New York after learning about the engagement in an attempt to talk Kismet out of what they viewed as a hasty marriage. But as soon as they met Andrew and saw the two of them together, they knew it was right. They didn't say another word against it.

A soft knock at my door at around midday lets me know they've arrived.

"Kismet, your parents are here," I say, but she doesn't stir. She hasn't willingly left the blanket cocoon she's made since building it. I wonder if she's even gone to the bathroom.

I open the door, and her mother greets me, red-eyed. She throws her arms around me, and I hug her back with one arm, smoothing her hair with my free hand as she weeps.

"Penn," Kismet's father says in greeting as he makes his way into my small apartment.

"Kismet's in the bedroom," I tell him through her mother's mass of blonde hair.

"I don't understand. They were so happy together." Her mother's sentiment strikes me as odd. She's acting as if their happiness somehow contributed to his death. I know she means that it only adds to the tragedy, but Andrew certainly didn't leave on purpose. I shake my head. If I've learned one thing over the past day, it's that people say odd things when they're grieving. It occurs to me that Kismet's mom is grieving for the life and love her daughter has lost more than she is for Andrew.

Eventually, she pulls herself together and moves away from me. "I'm sorry. It was a long night, having to be separated from her like that." I nod. I'm not sure what I would have done if I hadn't been able to be with Kismet last night. "How is she?"

"As you'd expect." I never know what to say when someone asks me that. The truth? She's terrible. Her true love just passed away. The other half of her soul is gone, leaving her to wander the Earth alone for the rest of her days.

"Has she started making arrangements?" her mother asks.

"No," I say simply. "It's only been a day."

"Yes, I know, but there's a lot to do. When we lost my mother, Kismet's grandma, the hospital was immediately pushing us to get the body out, and then the funeral home wanted her in the ground as soon as possible. It was hurry, hurry, hurry. At least I had help. My siblings were very involved, which was good, because my dad was a bit of a zombie through it all."

"Understandably so," I offer, and Kismet's mother nods in agreement.

"Kismet has us for that. Plus, the wedding will have to be..." She hesitates. "Disassembled. It's all so sad," she says as her voice quavers again. I brace myself for another outpouring of emotion, but she sniffs and holds back, thankfully.

"I need to see her," she says suddenly, sticking out her chin, as if that will help her be strong for her daughter.

I gesture toward the bedroom and follow her in. We find her dad sitting on the edge of the bed, silently rubbing her back. Her parents share a dark look as her mom walks around the bed.

"Kismet, sweetie. I'm here." She kneels by the bed, sweeping the hair away from her daughter's eyes. Tears fall silently down Kismet's face, and I fear they will continue to fall for an eternity.

ELEVEN

The days that follow are blanketed in a haze of grief that makes everything difficult to process. Aida stops by to offer help and bring food. Cody calls me, but we don't talk much. I appreciate the gesture, but I don't have anything to say, and Cody doesn't have any words, either, because when someone you love dies, there are none.

Kismet gets a lot of phone calls at first, but she never answers them. I try to field them for her, but after a while, I give up. Kismet knows people are trying, but she can't bring herself to respond to them. She can't bring herself to do much of anything.

Kismet's parents end up initiating the arrangements for Andrew, and I step in to help when important decisions are needed. I give her mother the key to their place, and she chooses some pictures for a slide show. When she asks me what song to use, I smile for the first time in days.

"I'm really tempted to tell you a song he would've hated, just to needle him one last time."

She smiles back. "You two were close, weren't you? You were going to be the best man?"

"We were like brothers," I say as I leaf through some of the pictures her mom picked out. They are all good. Andrew was very photogenic, and the love he and Kismet shared is so apparent in the photos they took together.

"Do you have any siblings? Family flying in to support you during the service?"

"I have two sisters, but they don't travel."

"That's a shame. Family is important at times like these."

"Kismet, Cedric, Aida, and Cody, they're my family now," I say, looking at the last picture in the pile. Andrew is young, a teenager. He stands on the end of a dock, holding a fish up that's as long as his torso. His grin is almost as big as the fish.

"He told me he fell in right after that was taken. The fish flopped and knocked him off balance. It got away in the end," Kismet says softly, her voice scratchy from disuse over the last few days.

I didn't even hear her come into the room. I pull out a seat for her, but she remains standing, as if she isn't sure she's ready to commit to joining us. Getting up was enough.

"Good to see you up, sweetie," her mom says, but Kismet doesn't respond. She just keeps looking at the picture of Andrew. A tear falls down her cheek, following a trail blazed by thousands of others.

I stretch my hand out to her, but she's just out of reach. She keeps her eyes fixed on the image. I hold the picture out to her, and she takes it from me, holding it close so she can study his face, as if she's afraid she'll forget what he looks like. The thought pours more grief into my already-full cup, but at least I've given her something solid to hold on to.

"The funeral is set for tomorrow, honey. Do you need me to go to the apartment to get you something to wear?" her mother asks. But she doesn't answer. Not because she doesn't want to, but because she doesn't hear. She's in her own world with Andrew.

"Yes, please do," I whisper to her mother, not wanting to interrupt her. I only have eyes for Kismet. Her beauty has been withered by grief. Her hair is a tangled mess, going every which direction, and greasy from days spent in bed. Her bloodshot, puffy eyes are exposed for the entire world to see. After raiding my closet, she's dressed in a sweatshirt that's two sizes too big and hangs off one shoulder, paired with sweat pants that are way too large and long. She looks like a rag doll.

"Okay," Kismet's mother softly says. "The wake starts at four, the service is at six, and there will be a graveside service to follow. So that'll give you plenty of time to get ready."

Kismet nods automatically, but I know she doesn't understand. How could she? I don't, and I'm a Fate. Or at least, I was.

That night, after Kismet's parents return to their hotel and Kismet settles into her cocoon, I lay on the floor beside her, wondering for the hundredth time what could have happened. The only heavenly person I know who seems capable of such a thing is Webber. It must have been him. But if his purpose was to get to me, why hurt Andrew? Why not Kismet? Webber knows how much I love her. Maybe he's toying with me. Maybe it's only a matter of time before he cuts her life's thread too. As I think of the damage Webber's doing to the tapestry, I'm filled with rage.

It's an emotion I haven't experienced to this degree before, and I'm not sure what to do. I leave the room, shutting the bedroom door behind me. Filled with energy, I pace the main room of the apartment as I try to puzzle out what I can do, how I can stop my rival from ruining the beauty of the human world. What did Webber say? *Dark threads add contrast to the tapestry*, or something like that. The thought of him weaving in black thread after black thread gives me chills, as does the realization that we're at his mercy now. All of us.

Surely, someone will see what he's doing. This can't go on for long. Maybe they already stopped him, and he's been punished. Maybe I will run into him on Earth. But that thought brings me up short. It doesn't make sense. Webber isn't the kind of guy to risk so much for so little gain. I have already been punished, and Webber has gotten exactly what he wants. What more does he stand to gain from killing Kismet's soul mate? Nothing, as far as I can tell. But I have no other answers.

I pace for a while longer, still at a loss. Then I think of Michaela. Is this why she was so upset the day I was banished?

Did she somehow see this coming? It's too upsetting to even consider.

"A Reaper," I say quietly to the dark room. "I have to find a Reaper."

Once I have a solution in mind, I'm able to settle down. I'm dozing off on the floor of my room when Kismet wakes me.

"Penn," she whispers.

Despite her quiet voice, she startles me. I've grown used to not hearing her speak, so I'm immediately on full alert. "What's wrong?" I sit up.

She's still lying with her back to me, and I can barely make out her shape.

"I need you to dye my dress black. I want to wear it tomorrow." The weight of what she says makes her voice thick.

"Of course." I get up immediately, pausing only to give her shoulder a squeeze. "I'll be downstairs if you need me. I just need to run to your apartment first."

She doesn't answer, and although I hope she's gone back to sleep, something tells me she's still awake. In fact, I question whether she's slept at all, which means she knows I've been up all night too. We're two tortured souls together, adrift in the night.

Once I return to the shop with her dress, I sigh as I set to work, darkening the threads of her dress, hoping her life's thread hasn't been darkened too.

The funeral is difficult to get through, not only because it's hard to see my friend, who was always the picture of health, lying there dead, but also because I'm so consumed by the need to find out what happened to him. I need answers, ones that might help save Kismet.

It's just a week from their scheduled wedding date, and Kismet is watching her fiancé lowered into the ground. The bride wears her wedding dress, forever blackened, and slouches over with sorrow. The life that's rightfully hers was stolen from her. And as I watch my dear friend return to the Earth, I make a silent vow to uncover the truth of what happened.

That night, after Kismet is back in her cocoon, I ask her parents to stay with her at my apartment. I tell them I have some digging to do.

"What kind of digging?" Kismet's dad asks once we're alone in the hallway outside my apartment. Her father is a kind man, but he can also sniff out bullshit from a mile away. Needless to say, he has zero tolerance for it.

"Honestly, I don't accept what happened to Andrew. I need to know more. I'm going to head to the hospital to see what I can find out."

"Penn, it's late. Anyone who can help you will have gone home hours ago. I understand that you're upset and you feel the need to take some kind of action, but this isn't the right way," Kismet's dad says, holding out his arm to usher me back into the apartment.

"This is just something I need to do. You're right, I probably won't be able to figure this out, but I need to try. I need to stay busy," I say, hoping that I've offered enough of the truth to satisfy him.

"Fine. I understand that," he says, shaking his head. He lowers his outstretched arm to shake my hand. "Good luck. If you don't find what you're looking for, I hope you at least find some peace."

I nod, shake the man's hand, and leave, heading straight for the closest hospital.

Reapers, like Michaela, are the only heavenly beings allowed to travel back and forth between the heavens and Earth. I have to go somewhere where people die, regularly. And the first idea that comes to mind is the ICU ward of the hospital.

So I catch the train over to Mount Sinai. It's well past dark when I arrive, and the hospital is pretty quiet. The receptionist at the front desk is both pleasant and helpful, and after smiling at me longer than is necessary, she directs me straight to the ICU ward. For the first time, I'm grateful for the immediate attraction women—and even some men—seem to have to me. It has helped me get past the first barrier.

As I ride the elevator to the correct floor, I wonder why I didn't think to try this sooner. Perhaps this will provide me with a connection to my other life. There are a lot of Reapers, so the odds are slim that I'll come across Michaela, but I really hope I do. Ultimately, she's the one I need to find. But perhaps another Reaper would be able to get a message to her. Anything is better than the questions that surround me now.

The doors open to the ICU ward, and I step out, but I don't get too far. The elevator dumps into the waiting room, staunchly guarded by the receptionist. The actual patients are securely kept behind doors that remain locked and tightly controlled by the woman at the desk. I approach cautiously, trying to come up with a feasible excuse to get past her.

Oh hi. I just need to make contact with a Reaper. I'll be out of your hair really fast, I promise. I shake my head. *Yes, do you have someone who's dying? Like right now? I'd like to linger at their bedside.* Maybe this isn't such a good idea after all.

"How can I help you?" the nurse asks. She's middle aged, with a blunt haircut and steel-rimmed glasses that perch at the end of her pointed nose, secured around her neck with a strand of pink beads. It seems to me she's all business, but at least she isn't openly hostile.

"My friend was brought here last week. He passed away. I think we might have left something of his behind. His fiancée asked me to come here and look around." The lie forms a little too easily, but I'm not really ashamed. Not much, anyway. I have to try. The means justify the ends, or at least I hope they will.

Removing her glasses from their perch, she studies me, and I catch a flash of sympathy in her gaze. But maybe I'm wrong. So many intact families come through that waiting room, only to leave broken. I wonder just how desensitized she is to my made-up plight.

"I am so sorry for your loss." Her tone is very genuine, and I decide she isn't too jaded, at least not yet. "However, I can't allow you to go into the ICU unless you are a direct family member of a patient. We can't have random people poking around in there. Perhaps you can tell me what room your friend was in, and I'll have an orderly look around. Although, I wouldn't hold my breath. The rooms are thoroughly cleaned after they are vacated."

Vacated. That's one way of putting it. Although I suppose not all patients vacate their rooms in the same way. In fact, a lot of them get better.

"Please, ma'am. Can you make an exception this one time? They were supposed to get married next week. She just wants this one last memento of him. I don't expect to find it, but I can't go home and tell her I didn't even look."

She crinkles her chin and frowns at me, as if sympathizing with my plight. "I'm sorry, but unfortunately, you aren't an exception." She looks over my shoulder at the families huddled in small groups behind me. "In times of tragedy, small things get forgotten. Things that aren't important when someone's life hangs in the balance can become monumental once they're gone." She looks back to me. "So unfortunately, you are the rule around here. The only advice I can give you is to go downstairs to look in the lost and found. You might have some luck. Frankly, I hope you do. There's too much bad news floating around here."

And with that, I'm dismissed. I nod my head, but I don't move right away—I can't bring myself to. My one chance at meeting a Reaper is so close, yet so far away. I look longingly at the doors behind the nurse, but she knows what I want.

"Have a nice day," she says firmly, letting me know it's beyond time for me to go.

Defeated, I go back to the elevator, unsure of what to do next, where to go. The odds of just happening on a car accident or someone dying so I can find a Reaper are so slim it's not even funny. Plus, with all these human emotions I'm feeling, I'm not sure I could handle something so gruesome. But what else can I do? As I walk out of the hospital, I spot the ER. But without an ailment, they won't let me past the waiting room there, either.

I leave the hospital with even more questions than I had before, and no conceivable way to answer them.

TWELVE

Kismet's parents stay around until a few days after the planned wedding day. Once the funeral is over, they start a campaign to try and get her to go home with them. There's nothing for her in New York, they say. It would be much better for her to go home and start fresh.

But even in her broken state, she knows that isn't true. She's been off work for two weeks, but her phone hasn't stopped ringing. Her face is still popping up around town—there are new posters on bus stops, buildings, and subway stations. She's on the cusp of something, and she knows it. The unshakable resolve that once dominated her personality fires to life when she tells them no. I see it again when she tells them no a second time. By the third time, she's adamant.

After they suggest it a fourth time, while we're having dinner on their last night in town, she says, "I agree with one thing you've said. I need to get out of our apartment."

Her parents both set their forks down in unison, making a clanging sound that echoes a bit in my small apartment.

"Kismet, it might be too soon for that," I say, eyeing her parents.

"I didn't say it has to be done today. I just said it has to be done."

"Where will you live?" Her mother's question comes out more like a demand.

"I'm not sure. Here, for now, if that's okay with Penn."

Her mother frowns, clearly disapproving of her choice.

A sense of dread fills me as I watch Kismet stare long and hard at her mother. Whatever is said at this table will be damaging for a long time. I can feel it hanging in the air. But there's nothing I can say to stop it. Whatever I do will be used as more ammunition in their battle.

So I sit silently, watching in horror as the two women stare each other down, each biting back what she wants to say. Finally, her mother lets it go. "Don't you think you've settled into another man's home awfully fast?"

"Wow, Mom. That's below the belt, don't you think?" Kismet's tone is cold and emotionless, and it scares me. She's always been so positive and upbeat. I don't like where this conversation is going at all. I look desperately to her dad for rescue, or at least guidance, but judging from the look on his face, he agrees with his wife.

Kismet's mother sits staring at her, her lips pinched together, as if she's holding back another sharp comment.

Kismet throws up her hands and lets out an exasperated breath. "I haven't *settled* in to anything, Mom. For heaven's sake. It's been less than a week, and all I know for sure is I can't sleep in that apartment anymore. Ever. It's where my life was supposed to be, and now it's not. I don't need to be reminded of that every time I go through my front door. And I don't need *you* judging me for that."

"Honey, that's *not* what we're judging you for." Her mom slams her mouth shut, as if she regrets the words as soon as they're out.

"What your mother means is that your feelings are totally understandable." Finally, her dad jumps into the conversation. "Of course you don't want to be in the home you were supposed to share with Andrew. But wouldn't you rather spend this time supported by your family, rather than by Andrew's best friend? Don't you think you've burdened him enough?"

I can't stay silent any longer. "Whoa, hold on. Don't bring me into this. Kismet isn't a burden under any circumstance. Frankly, I'm a bit rattled by this whole thing myself, and I've appreciated having some company around." Blood is pounding in my ears. I'm getting upset, but I'm not sure why. Is it because they're trying to take Kismet away from me? Or because they're acting like she's some harlot who's jumped from Andrew's bed to mine in one fell swoop? I shake my head. The more I think about it, the angrier I get.

"You raised her better than that, by the way," I add. "You should also know her better than that. What would ever make you think she would cast Andrew aside so easily? I would never have introduced the two of them if I thought for as single second they weren't worthy of each other." I pause, taking a moment to look at each of her parents in turn. Their horrified expressions slightly soften my anger.

"Look, I know you're just trying to help, to be supportive," I continue. "But your words are hurting her. And you're not exactly painting me in a flattering light, either. So why not try to trust your daughter? She's done well for herself so far. If you doubt that, go see one of her plays when she gets back to work."

They both look away, and then at each other.

"Why not stay with one of your girlfriends? Someone from the play perhaps?" her mom persists. "People will talk, Kismet."

"So *what*?" Kismet shouts. "My fiancé died days before we were supposed to get married. People already thought I was pregnant because we supposedly rushed into the wedding. Now think how they'll talk. I'm all alone and knocked up."

"You're not, though, right?" her mom asks. At that moment, I don't think the conversation can get any worse. The looming sense of dread I feel makes me shift in my seat.

"Mom, Penn's right. You've lost sight of who I am. If you knew, you wouldn't even need to ask that question. And really, would that be such a terrible thing? I'd have a piece of him with me, as long as I lived. And you'd have a grandchild. What would be so bad about that?"

"But…" her mom persists.

"No, Mom. You're not going to be a grandma, so let it go." Silence weighs heavily on the four of us as we sit around the dinner table. Our food has long since gone cold, but we all toy with it, pushing it around as if trying to unbury just the right thing to say.

We're all good people, so what went wrong? Why is Kismet's family crumbling right in front of me?

"Okay, let's just take a deep breath," I venture one last time. "We all want what's best for Kismet. So if we can keep that in mind, and trust her to make her own decisions, everything will be fine."

But my words don't help at all. Her dad pushes back from the table and stands. "You've known my daughter for how long? A few months? And you presume to know her better than her own father?"

That's not what I meant to say at all, but it's too late. Her mother is standing too.

"Kismet, I can't force you to come home with us tomorrow. Nor, it seems, can I force you to make the right choices about Penn, here. But I do wish you would reconsider."

"Duly noted, Daddy," she says, but she remains seated.

"I hope to see you at the airport tomorrow. We'll buy you a ticket tonight, just in case," he says.

"That won't be necessary, but thank you for the gesture."

"Kismet, please," her mother pleads.

"Bye, Mom. Have a safe trip," Kismet says. With that, she stands up. But instead of hugging her parents goodbye, she grabs her plate and carries it to the sink, turning her back on the people who've loved her most her whole life. It breaks what's left of my heart.

"I'll walk you out," I say, and they don't object.

Once they're in the hallway, I try to repair some of the damage I've caused. "I apologize if I overstepped. Obviously, you know her better than I do. But you need to understand that she and I are not romantically involved. We never were, and in light of what's happened, I don't think we ever will be. Neither of us will ever get over what happened to Andrew. But it's a shared trauma, something we've bonded over. She doesn't have to explain it to me, and I don't have to explain it to her. Please, just try to be supportive as she attempts to move forward with her life. If she can manage that, she'll do great things. I know it."

Neither of them responds. They just nod curtly and turn to leave.

"Have a safe flight, guys. Thank you for everything," I say to their backs as they walk away. Only her father turns and nods in acknowledgment of my gratitude.

When I go back inside, I find Kismet at the sink, shaking. She's holding a plate in her hands, poised to put it in, but it hovers just shy of the bottom.

"How dare they," she says, more matter-of-factly than accusingly, and finally sets the plate down in the sink. "How *dare* they." The second time is much more emotional, and I can tell her mood is escalating.

But it doesn't end the way I expected it would. Instead of railing about their misunderstanding and lack of support, she turns to look at me with fire in her eyes, fire that's quickly extinguished by a burst of tears. All I can do is take her in my arms.

"I miss him so much," she says through her sobs. "None of this should be happening. We should be at the Four Seasons right now, saddle sore from all of our newlywed shenanigans."

I chuckle, but it's a sad sound. "Yeah, I don't need all the honeymoon details."

"It's not fair," she cries out. By that point, my shirt is soaked through with her tears.

"No. It's not." It's all I can say, because she's right. It isn't fair.

I don't give up on finding a Reaper. I find myself frequenting nursing homes on the rare occasions when I don't have to work and Kismet is busy.

Now that Kismet's parents are gone, she's eager for something to do, so she goes back to the diner, and tells her director she's ready to pretend she's someone else.

I'm worried at first, but when I go to her first show a few weeks later, she's better than ever. She immerses herself in the character in a way she never has before, as if she truly is that person. Maybe for those few hours she's on stage, it's true. She leaves the tragic woman she's become behind and blossoms into the heroine of a new story. It's absolute magic, and I only wish Andrew could be there to see it.

After Kismet goes back to work, I have more time to focus on getting some answers. I need to protect her. I start wondering who else has been banished and where they might be. Maybe a fallen angel might be able to cast some light on what's happening.

A quick Google search for fallen angels plants a seed of doubt into my brilliant plan. Although there isn't much information, no one gets thrown from heaven for being good. Some of the angels were cast out for wanting God's power. Still others were cast out for descending from the heavens and seducing the people on Earth. Watchers, they're called. They sound less dangerous.

I've never heard of a Watcher before. But that may be because they don't live in the heavens anymore; they've all been cast out. I wonder at the reliability of human information on the heavens, but I can't afford to be picky. It's all I have to go on.

I have to find a Watcher, if they exist. But where should I start looking? Most of the sources I find claim the Watchers descended to Mount Hermon and wreaked havoc from there. Maybe one or two still hang around that area. It's a long shot, but it's my best lead. I just have to sell it to Kismet.

I've decided to ask Kismet to go with me. Even though it'll be difficult to do what needs to be done without rousing her suspicions, I need to keep an eye on her.

When she gets home from rehearsal that night, I broach the subject. "Kismet, I'd like to take a trip. Together."

"Oh? Where?" she asks distractedly as she takes off her shoes and sets her purse and keys on the small table near the door.

"Syria, I think."

She laughs. "Syria. That's very specific. Also, I'm not sure the Middle East is the best place to go right now. Aren't they at war? I'm not big on trying to get into a country that so many people are trying to get out of. Anyway, I just went back to work."

She sits down on the couch next to me as if it's a closed subject. "Still. I'd like to try," I say.

I have no idea how my plan will work. I have a passport now, thanks to Cedric, but the idea of testing it makes me nervous. Traveling to a war-torn country where security is tight seems like asking for trouble.

Sinking back into the couch, I reconsider my idea. "Maybe you're right," I say, letting my disappointment come through more than I intended.

She looks at me then, as if taking my inquiry seriously for the first time. "You were serious about going to Syria?"

"No. It was a dumb idea. I'll find another way."

"Another way to what?" she asks, but I don't answer her. Instead, I head back to the computer, intent on brainstorming more ways to find a Watcher.

What are the odds that one of them has made their way to New York City? Without knowing exactly how many Watchers there originally were, I can't figure the number exactly, but I'm guessing the chances are pretty slim.

What else can I do? In the meantime, maybe I'll think of a better idea, but for now, I'll start my search in New York.

My progress is slow, mostly because my attention is so divided. Between resuming my work at the shop and trying to be supportive of Kismet, the months that follow Andrew's death don't offer many opportunities to find a Watcher.

I find myself going to all of Kismet's plays, in a way I never did when Andrew was alive. After all, that was his responsibility. We never turn down an opportunity to meet for lunch or dinner. Somewhere along the line, the friendly hugs change. Kismet starts to linger longer than normal, and I let myself breathe in her scent—lavender, with a touch of lemon.

I'm already in love with her; I have been for a while. But it's all new for her, and it scares both of us, so we ignore it for quite some time. Months pass this way. We spend more and more time together, our casual affections growing more frequent.

In that time, I struggle to maintain my focus. It's a struggle, though, and Kismet starts to occupy my mind more and more. The drive to find answers is replaced by the need to make Kismet happy, to see her smile again. And the more she leans on me, the stronger that need grows.

As the months pass, I only find time to steal away on occasion to conduct my search, making the quest for answers frustratingly slow. I start out at the churches and temples, asking the priests what they know about Watchers, or fallen angels. Most have never heard them referred to as Watchers.

Eventually, my search brings me to Rabbi Frankel.

His temple is built from stone and colored glass, and the big, wooden doors creak loudly when I go inside.

The man is in an office, sleeping behind a large, wooden desk covered in open books and papers scrawled in shaky handwriting. He's an old rabbi, and he looks hunched down under the weight of his congregation's burdens. I clear my throat as I gently knock on the doorframe.

"Excuse me, Rabbi Frankel. My name is Penn. I have a few questions for you if you have a moment."

The rabbi wakes slowly, his salt-and-pepper beard draping down over his chest, and his feet perch on the desk in front of him. "Hmm?"

"I have a few questions, if you have a moment," I say again.

"What? Oh certainly, my boy. Please, come in, sit down." He sits up without hurrying, and he doesn't try to apologize for the fact that he was sleeping. I like him already.

I take the chair across from his desk as he closes a few of the books in front of him, but it seems like his heart isn't in the effort, as he leaves most of them open. He notices me watching him. "I'd hate to lose my place. It's hard enough to get started without a bone-headed move like that."

I smile. "Well, don't feel any pressure to tidy up on my account. I've interrupted your nap."

"Yes, you did. So this better be important." The rabbi has a glint of mischief in his eye, making me smile broadly.

"I was wondering if you'd ever heard of a Watcher."

"Like a fallen angel?"

"Yes."

"Well, since I knew what you meant, yes, I've heard of them. Why?"

"I'd like to find one."

The rabbi leans forward on his desk, staring intently at me. I have the old man's attention now, and all traces of sleep are gone. His gaze is sharp and intense, and I know intuitively that if I don't watch what I say around this man, my secret will be out.

"What an interesting idea. I'd never considered that they might still be around. But why not? It's safe to assume angels are immortal. So why wouldn't they still be wandering the Earth?" Something about the way he says it makes me feel like he's teasing me, like he knows more than he's letting on.

Before I can pursue it, he gets to his feet and circles to the huge shelf of books to my right. He pulls one out and brings it to my side of the desk, gesturing for me to come closer. After opening the book to a specific page, he begins reading aloud.

"Abaddon was said to be the most notorious Watcher. He was known for turning even the most loyal women away from their husbands. One woman in particular was well known in her village for deeply loving her husband. Knowing this, Abaddon took it as a challenge. At first, she resisted, suspecting who, and what, he was. But he disguised himself as her husband, and she lay with him. She was so distraught that she threw herself in the river. Shortly after that, the Watchers were cast out of heaven."

"Does it say where that was?" I ask, wanting to take the text from the man to search it for myself.

"No. It doesn't. But this was millennia ago. I can't imagine an angel like that would stay in one place for long."

"Do you think there could be Watchers here in New York?"

That question gives the old man pause. "Why do you need to find one so bad?"

"I need to make a connection with the heavens."

"My dear boy. Just pray. That's the easiest way to connect."

For humans. Yes. But I'm not human. And I'm also banished. My prayers will fall on deaf ears, and I know it. "My prayers won't be answered. I need another way."

Sadness creeps in to the old man's expression. "Perhaps you're not listening hard enough."

"Rabbi, I don't need to be saved. I am fine really. I just want to…" I hesitate. To what? "Find answers."

"And you think an upstanding citizen like a Watcher is going to help you?" The old man's eyes crinkle at the outside corners with the joys of years past when he smiles.

"Okay, so it might not be the most ideal plan, but it's the best one I've got. My other option didn't work, and I'm running out of ideas." I know I've said too much, but I'm frustrated. It's been months since Andrew died, and my search has yielded nothing.

"A friend of mine died unexpectedly. He shouldn't have. He was supposed to have a long and healthy life. Something is wrong, and I need to know what. More than that, I need to make sure it won't happen to Kismet."

"Kismet. What a lovely name."

Of course, that's the detail he zeros in on. I hadn't even intended to say her name.

"If death is what you seek, why not find the angel of death?"

I watch the man closely, choosing my words carefully. "I tried. They wouldn't let me into the ICU."

"Ah. I see. So a Watcher was your next best option?" The old man raises a very hairy eyebrow at me.

"Well, do you have any better ideas?"

"Yes. Pray. I told you that already."

"And I heard you. Perhaps a more actionable approach would be helpful."

"My boy, I find nothing more actionable than the power of prayer."

I frown. There's no way to make this human understand, and besides, the man clearly has no idea where to find a Watcher. So, I stand. "Thank you for your time, Rabbi." I hold out my hand for the man to shake, but he only stares at it.

"Sit down, for heaven's sake. We're not done."

I plant my butt back in the chair like a cowed child.

"Now, modern times would have been kind to the Watchers. Adultery isn't as frowned upon as it once was. Although the challenge is gone, the carnal need can be met with an overwhelming amount of supply."

I shift in my seat, uncomfortable talking about such an intimate topic with a rabbi. "I don't think a strip club is where I'd start. You need something more high class. A brothel maybe? Or an escort service? But you're not looking for an employee. You're looking for the owner."

My face lights up with the sheer brilliance of the idea. "Not all brothel owners will be fallen angels," I say, as my mind races at the possibilities. For the first time in months, I have a lead, an idea that might work.

"I must caution you in your pursuit, my friend. If you care for this Kismet, are you willing to sacrifice her in your quest for answers? If you really do find a Watcher, she would make a fine prize for him."

I sit back in my chair heavily, feeling totally defeated.

"Weigh your options carefully before you go any further. There are no choices without consequences."

I look at him, wondering not for the first time how much he truly understands.

The rabbi leans back in his chair and returns his feet to the desktop, making himself comfortable, then drags a book into his lap and opens it. "Perhaps another option might be more appealing to you," he says, eyeing me over the top of his book.

"I'm not praying if that's what you're going to suggest again."

He smiles sadly at me. "Although I still think it's worth a shot, that's not what I was going to say." He leans forward and pushes a few books aside, uncovering a phone on his desk.

Pressing a button, he asks, "Can you come in here for a moment, please?"

"Of course," a woman's voice answers. Even over the phone, I can tell she's special. Her voice sings. Something about it tugs at my memory, making my pulse quicken.

Not five seconds later, an old woman appears in the doorframe. Her long, silvery hair is pulled away from her face in a loose bun, with strands tumbling down every which way. She seems elderly, but she stands up straight as a rail, not at all burdened by the passing of the years. Her skin is weathered, but her eyes are crystal clear. They're so familiar to me that I almost stand and go to her.

She gasps at the sight of me, but then she clears her throat and says, "Yes, Rabbi, how can I help you?"

He smiles, quite pleased with himself. "Fia. I believe you can help this boy."

She nods, but neither of us is capable of movement. *Fia.* Can it be? She looks so much older than when I knew her, but the eyes...

Slowly I stand. "But... the Keeper said..."

Her stern look makes me clamp my mouth shut before I can say any more. She holds her arm out. "Right this way, young man."

"Have fun, you two," the rabbi says, and I can tell by the sound of his voice, he's barely holding back a laugh.

She shuts her office door behind her, and then wraps me up in the biggest hug I've had since landing on Earth. Aida gives some good hugs, but this, this one is filled with memories of times long since passed.

"I thought I'd never see you again," we both whisper.

"What are you doing here?" we say together.

Laughing, she leads me to a chair in front of her desk. Her office is similar to the Rabbi's, but smaller. I sit in a small, red leather armchair, and she chooses to sit next to me rather than taking the seat behind her desk.

"You go first," she instructs.

I spend the next hour telling her everything. About Kismet,

the day I made her, how I fell, Michaela's mysterious problem, Andrew's untimely death, and my suspicions about Webber. She doesn't interrupt me the entire time, and I'm so happy to get it all out, I'm nearly crying by the end.

When I'm finished, I realize she's resting her hand on mine, although I have no memory of her putting it there.

"Well, that's quite a tale, Penn. I leave you alone for a few centuries, and you let the whole world go to hell, huh?" A smile pulls at the corner of her mouth as she gets up and goes to the corner of her office, where she pours two cups of tea.

She hands one of the cups to me. "I retired here centuries ago, shortly after you took over. I move around a lot to avoid suspicion. I found Rabbi Frankel about twenty years ago. He knows some of who I am. I don't think he knows I was a Fate, but he certainly knows I came from the heavens."

"I gathered that," I say, thinking of his knowing smiles as I sip the hot tea. The weather is getting colder, and it feels good in my cold hands. "Why the aged appearance?" I ask. "I almost didn't recognize you. The eyes give you away."

"It draws less attention. Plus, people would notice quickly if I didn't seem to age."

Thinking of how much attention my appearance has garnered since I arrived on Earth, I understand completely. The possibility of aging my appearance never even occurred to me, but it's brilliant. The perfect way to blend in among the humans.

"You stand up too straight," I say, gesturing to her back. "Someone as old as you've made yourself look wouldn't have such good posture."

"Well, I didn't ask you for your opinion, did I, newbie?" she says, raising an eyebrow at me before she sips her tea. I've come home, or so it feels. We're back to our easy banter from the days before I became an official Fate.

After a few moments of silence, I ask her. "Can you go back?" There's an ounce of hope in my voice. She could be my connection to Michaela.

"No. I'm sorry, I can't. I've retired here for good."

"So... how is banishment different from retirement?" I ask.

"I chose this. I spent some time researching what life was like on Earth, studying the humans. I also got plenty of resources. I wasn't left penniless and naked like you were. I have everything I need to live comfortably forever."

I sit back in my chair. "So what do you think is happening?"

"Whatever it is doesn't sound good. I've never met most of the people you're talking about, so I don't have much of a point of reference. But I do know that if Reapers don't want to see you, you won't see them. I agree that getting in touch with Michaela is the most direct way you can get answers, but the only way you'll accomplish that is if she comes to you. Seeking her out is a waste of your time."

I snort. "Clearly."

"I also think finding a Watcher is a very bad idea. They won't help you. They're the most selfish souls around. And they'll take you for everything you're worth. Kismet is no exception."

"So what are you saying? You think I should just sit and wait?" I say, not at all pleased with this prospect.

"Maybe. You never were very patient."

"It's not about patience, Fia. Kismet and Andrew are connected. How do I know she won't follow him to the grave? I'm not sure I can afford to sit here and do nothing."

"I'm not sure you have much of a choice right now. I don't think this is your time to act," Fia answers.

"How can you possibly know that?" I ask, hoping she still has a connection to the heavens.

"I don't. But I do know God. And although this might seem out of control for us, it's not for Him. He will use you to rein this problem in when the time is right."

I think about some of His last words to me. *I'm not through with you yet, Penn*, his voice echoes in my mind.

"I just hope He does it before anything more unravels."

Time marches on, as it tends to do. Fia and I see each other regularly. To explain our connection to Kismet, Fia has claimed the title of my mother's aunt. I don't know where she comes up with these things, but Kismet has welcomed her into our lives with open arms, excited to have a connection to my family, and my past.

Easily, we fall into a routine of dinners with Fia every other week, dancing around the rest of our obligations. The girls' favorite pastime during these shared meals becomes swapping embarrassing stories about me. Fia, of course, changes any heavenly details, but it does nothing to wipe the memories of my embarrassments.

"My sisters weren't too keen on Penn. When he was a young boy, he liked to come to work and poke around. Oh, he was always getting himself into trouble. One time, he asked my sister if she had such a sour face because she'd eaten a lemon. I nearly died. She didn't think it was all that funny."

Kismet dissolved into giggles, and the sound filled my soul with joy. What was a little embarrassment if it got her laughing?

It's hard to accept, but I know Fia's right. I can only wait for now. When the time comes to act, I'll know what to do.

One night, just before Christmas, Kismet asks me for something. "Penn, I'd like you to go to the cemetery with me."

I look up from my book, startled to see that she's fully dressed in a coat, scarf, hat, and mittens. Closing my book, I stand. "Sure, Kismet. Just let me get my coat."

We walk the entire way, not speaking. Kismet hooks her arm in mine, and I stuff my hands in my pockets to try and keep warm. The snow drifts lazily to the ground, and the lights everywhere give the city a magical feel. Although it's getting late, I don't mind being out when it's this lovely.

We round the last corner, automatically finding the way to Andrew's resting place. I often visit my dear friend to tell him about Kismet and life at the store. But I rarely go with Kismet. She likes to go on her own, and I understand that.

When we arrive, I brush the snow off his gravestone. The simple marker stands out among the big, flashy ones that surround it. It states his name, dates of birth and death, and is etched with a simple statement: *You are missed*. It has been almost six months since his death, but I still have trouble imagining my life without him. The ache remains keen.

Once I'm done clearing away the snow, and we can both see the writing, Kismet says, "All right boys, we need to talk." There's an authoritative tone in her voice that I haven't heard in months.

I look at her curiously, a half smile on my face. "I think you'll find the conversation a bit one-sided," I say, earning a fierce look. Whatever Kismet has on her mind, it's serious.

"I've been struggling a lot with what I want to say, but in the end, I know you both want me to be happy. That's all you've ever wanted."

I shift my weight as I stand on one corner of this strange triangle we've formed. I can't help but wonder where she's going with this.

"Andrew, I love you. I always will. But you're not here with me anymore. You won't ever be." Her voice hitches. "We can't have the life we planned, so I need to move on."

What does she mean? Is she planning to move out? I'm not sure how I feel about that. Admittedly, I'm tired of sleeping on the floor, but I bought an air mattress when I realized she wasn't going anywhere. And I cleared some space in the apartment for her belongings after she moved out of theirs—and sold most of their stuff—a few months ago.

Panic sets in as a new idea occurs to me. Is she thinking about moving back to Florida to be with her parents? Has the strain of Andrew's death been too much? If she does leave, I'm not sure how I'll cope with having her so far away.

"Andrew, I know you loved Penn like a brother. I did too, actually. He set his own feelings aside because he saw what was best for both of us. How could you not love someone like that?" She pauses, waiting for him to respond. The wind gently blows a snowflake onto her nose, and she laughs. It's a sound I don't hear much anymore, and it delights me. I reach out for her hand, and she takes it.

Looking deep into my eyes, she goes on. "I'm in love with Penn, Andrew. And I think you would approve. Because I know you loved him too." Her words make me lightheaded, and my smile feels broad enough to carry me off on a slight breeze.

Although I knew her feelings for me have been changing, it's still startling to hear her say the words out loud, especially in front of her fiancé's grave. But I know she's done it on purpose, as if to get his approval. Or maybe to unburden herself. Either way, she has declared her love for me, and it takes my breath away.

She looks up at me with glittering green eyes that are filled with tears—I'm not sure if they're tears of happiness or sadness, but something tells me they're both. I cradle her face in one hand, and her hand in the other.

"I'm not sure you will ever understand just how special you are, but if you'll let me, I would like to spend your whole life telling you," I say, and she leans in and kisses me, throwing her arms around my neck.

At first, I just stand there, drinking her in as our lips connect. But the joy I feel begs to be expressed. I lift her up, and we spin as the snow swirls around us.

When we both get a little dizzy, we separate and I put her down.

"Good. I'm glad you're on the same page," Kismet says.

"Honey, I've been on this page since I first saw you."

She smiles and turns to face Andrew's headstone. "Goodnight, my love. I hope you are happy. I've decided to be." She squeezes my hand as she turns, and we walk together out of the cemetery.

———————

That night, I don't lay on the floor. Kismet doesn't let go of my hand once as she leads me straight through the apartment to the bedroom. She only releases it when we reach the end of the bed, and only then, so she can shed her coat and start unbuttoning her blouse.

I swallow hard. Are we really going to do this? I reach up and grab her hand. "We don't have to do this tonight."

But rather than be deterred by my comment, she smiles and

presses on. "I know," she says, as if I should know that too.

She moves slowly, purposefully, and I let her take the lead. I'm in over my head, and I'm not sure if she's the water washing over me, or the life preserver that will save me. Either way, I cling to her as she slowly undresses me, fully revealing my body to her for the first time. I've never been with a woman before— it isn't something we felt the need to do in the heavens.

Apparently, my nerves are unwarranted, for she gasps at the sight of my chiseled body. "Good God, you're gorgeous."

I don't respond. I'm too busy drinking in the sight of her. Although I know her better than anyone on Earth, I've never known her like *this*. When I see her naked in front of me, it stirs feelings I wasn't sure I was capable of experiencing. I don't just love her. I *want* her.

As she trails kisses along my body, she carries me to new heights of ecstasy. Then she pulls me down to the bed, and the passion and love and connection that has been building between us ignites.

Late that night, she sleeps with her head snuggled up to my chest. I stroke her long, brown hair, breathe in the scent of her lavender shampoo, and wonder how banishment could be so bittersweet.

THIRTEEN

Our life together isn't easy, that's for sure. We aren't soul mates, so we don't understand each other's needs on that deeper level. We fight more than I ever saw Kismet and Andrew fight. But I love her more than anything on Earth or in the heavens. And I think Kismet loves me as well as she can love a man who isn't her soul mate. So, we do our best. Some days, we knock it out of the park, most days in fact, but we also stumble. Some days, we don't find the right words. Sometimes, we have to start fresh the next morning. But that's fine with me, because no matter what, we always start over.

The months go by in a flash. I mark my first anniversary on Earth by having dinner with Aida, Cody, and their kids while Kismet is busy rehearsing for a new play on Broadway. I'm grateful there's no talk of the day we met, or the reason for the occasion. They've long since learned there are some questions I can't, and won't, answer. But we share one another's company in a way that reminds me of how these people have come to my rescue in every possible way.

A few months later, we mark the one-year anniversary of Andrew's death. It's a hard day for everyone, and I'm reminded that even though a year has slipped away, I still have no idea what happened to my friend.

Fia reminds me regularly to be patient.

"You have to admit, this isn't right, Fia. In all my years as a Fate, nothing like this ever happened. Threads aren't supposed to snap on their own. This goes against *everything* we know to be true," I say into the phone as I pace around the living room. Kismet is in the shower, so this is my chance to be blunt.

"You're right. It does. I've been thinking about it a lot. I've been here on Earth for a long time, and I've met a lot of different people. Last century, my best friend fancied herself to be a witch of sorts. She said she could travel between the world of the living and the dead. Now, I didn't believe her for a minute, but she did know some things. She knew someone helped souls cross over. She referred to a 'tapestry of life,' but not in quite the correct context."

"But, if you knew her last century, isn't she long dead?"

"Yes. She was the last in her family of witches, as they called themselves. She didn't have a daughter. But her knowledge may not be dead. Or perhaps you could find another clan somewhere. If the ability to go back and forth really does exist, that could be your ticket to answers."

I sigh. It is a bit of a long shot. "I'm worried, Fia."

"Worry is a human emotion, Penn. We have more faith than to stoop to it."

"We're also used to having more control," I say, my frustration mounting. "Fia, it's been a year."

"That should help you feel better that Kismet is safe."

"Kismet is no safer today than she was a year ago."

"What do you mean by that?" Kismet's voice halts my pacing mid-step. I slowly turn to face her. She's wrapped in a towel, using another to dry her hair.

"Shit," I mumble under my breath.

"You are far too human, dear Fate," Fia scolds. Heavenly beings don't swear ever, which probably makes my curse all the more shocking to her.

"Fia, I'll call you later." I hang up before she can respond, but I know she's shaking her head.

"What's going on? Why do you think I'm in danger?" Kismet asks, and I can tell she's not sure if she should be worried.

"I..." I trail off, frantically trying to come up with a response.

"Penn. What's going on?"

I turn to her and take both of her hands in mine. "You know what? It's nothing that you need to worry about."

"What does that mean? That I'm too stupid to understand?" I know that tone—she's confused, so she's reaching for her insecurities to make sense of what I've said.

"No. That's not what I meant at all." But how can I convince her of that without telling her the truth, and not just some of the truth, but all of it?

"So..." She lets the word hang for a moment or two. "What did you mean?"

"I just don't want to stress you out with something silly, that's all."

"Me being in danger doesn't sound like something silly. In fact, it sounds like the perfect thing to worry about. Either I should be worried about me and my safety or I should be worried about you and whether or not you've lost your mind."

I sigh, getting exasperated. "No. That's—"

She cuts me off. "You can't talk to me about it, but you can tell Fia? She's somehow worthier of this secret than I am?"

"No. Fia is family." As soon as it's out of my mouth, I know it's the wrong thing to say.

"And I'm not?" She folds her hands over her chest, the anger building in her eyes.

Honestly, I don't feel like I can make this any worse. But then I consider the consequences of telling her the truth. Fia and I have discussed the possible fallout of telling the humans who we are. Fia thinks they wouldn't be able to handle it. She argues it's better, and easier, to keep it secret. But the Rabbi is living proof that she's not altogether right. Besides, Fia is also single, and she has been for centuries. She says that's easier too, and she likes to mock me for my "tender heart."

But then I think of the consequences. Will there be retribution from the heavens? Or maybe the greater risk is that Kismet will just think I'm nuts. She might leave.

As she watches me war with myself, I try to come up with an answer that will satisfy her. But none of those things lead up to the truth. And from my own search for answers, I know how hard it is to settle for anything less.

"Can I ask you something?" Kismet says, her voice softening a little. "That night in the cemetery, you said you would love me for as long as I live. I've got to tell you, that creeped me out a little. You planning on killing me?"

I laugh out loud. "No. Absolutely not."

"Does that have something to do with why you never talk about your past? Your family? I hoped you'd open up more after you found Fia, but it hasn't happened. She's as guarded as you are. And you share your secrets with her; I know you do. I feel more excluded than ever. Whatever you're a part of, though, she's a part of it too." Each sentence comes out faster than the last. She's piecing it together right in front of my eyes. Paralyzed with fear or maybe excitement, I sit there and listen as she tries to tell me my secret.

"Are you in some kind of cult with her?"

Again, I laugh. It's sort of close, yet so far from the truth. "No, I can definitively tell you that I am not in a cult with Fia." Secretly, I wish she were on speakerphone. She would be dying laughing.

"What then? What have you been keeping from me all this time? Don't you want to unburden yourself?"

I squeeze her hands. "Yes. I want to unburden myself. I'm sure Andrew told you about asking me about my past that night on your back deck. I wanted to tell him. I wanted to share my story after Cody and Aida rescued me without any expectations or questions. I felt like I owed it to them, and I *especially* feel like I owe it to you. But I don't know what the rules are. And I've already made mistakes that cost a life. I won't gamble with yours when I don't fully understand what the consequences of that gamble might be."

"You did what? Did you kill someone?" Her face goes pale.

I sigh. This is sounding bad, even to my ears. "Not on purpose, no."

"Did you do time? Is that why you won't talk about your past?"

"No, I'm doing my time now."

She crinkles her eyebrows, creating a deep wrinkle between them as she tries to decipher what I've said. "You don't wear an ankle cuff or anything like that. What do you mean—you're doing your time now?"

I sigh, deciding to try one last diversion. "Kismet, I love you. I sacrificed my entire way of life to be with you in any capacity. I knew you were meant to be with Andrew, so I never imagined we would be together the way we are now. When I went to the diner that day, I just wanted to see you. To say goodbye, I guess. Get some closure. But after I met you in the flesh, I couldn't bear to step away from your life. Andrew wasn't supposed to die. Fia is helping me search for answers. That's all."

There, I think. I hope it's just enough of the truth for her to let it go. But it only creates more questions.

"Answers? What kind of answers? Any time someone dies young, there are no answers."

I nod. "Yes, you're right. I need to let it go. I'm just having trouble doing that." I hope the tiny lie will push her away from the subject. But she circles back around, latching onto one of the details I mentioned.

"We met for the first time at the diner. How could you possibly have been in love with me before that?"

I know I can create some story about falling in love with her after watching *Madame Curie*, but I don't want to lie. Not tonight.

"Can we please let this go?" I say. "I've already told you more than I'm comfortable sharing. I have no idea what the consequences would be if I were to tell you everything. You'd probably leave me for being a total whack job."

She releases my hand and folds her arms over her chest, giving me a look that says, 'try me.'

I feel trapped. Intuition tells me this secret will destroy our relationship from the inside. I haven't done a good enough job of hiding it. The closer we get, the more of myself I reveal to her. Tonight, I actually talked to Fia about going on a witch-hunt while Kismet was still in the apartment.

I sigh. I started this ball rolling months ago. The consequences will be what they are. It's time to come clean.

"If you decide to leave me tonight, know that I love you with my entire being. That is what this has always been about for me."

She holds her challenging stance, and I can tell she thinks I'm bullshitting her. With nothing left to do but plow forward, I say, "I am a Spinner. You know that. But you don't know all of it. I was the Spinner of the Fates. When I lived in the heavens, I spun the thread of life. My two sisters, whom you've only heard me speak of once or twice, are the other two Fates. Horatia, the one who cuts the thread, and Galenia, the one who decides how each person will die. That's who they are. I was banished from the heavens shortly after creating you and Andrew. You were special, a sparkling thread among billions of dull ones, and you created a beautiful shining spot in the tapestry of life. Andrew was your complement in every way. Your life together should have been perfect. I watched Horatia cut your threads, and they were both extraordinarily long. Andrew's death was an anomaly. He should've lived just as long as you. Because I don't understand what happened; I'm worried you might be in danger." Once it's out, I expect to feel a huge sense of relief, but I don't. I am consumed with dread when I think about the words that are currently trapped behind her tongue.

"I… um…" She struggles, clearly not sure where to start. Sinking down to the floor, she sits at my feet. Her own are tucked under her. Reaching for her hands, I sit down facing her. I take it as a good sign when she doesn't pull away.

"Assuming all of this is true, why were you banished? Does it have something to do with the person you killed?"

I will never cease to be amazed by her intelligence… by the way she pieces things together on her own. "Yes. I couldn't get over you. I couldn't stop thinking about you. I connected with you in a way I'd never connected with anyone before. I watched you grow, knowing what an amazing life you had in store for you. It only made my love for you grow stronger. The truth is, I couldn't move on. After I created Andrew for you, I felt like I'd peaked, like I had nothing left to give. I made others, but I wasn't as productive, and the work meant nothing to me. After a while, I grew impatient and tried to force a creation. It was wrong, and I knew it, but I didn't want to accept the truth. That life ended up being a stillborn—an unordered stillborn. A wasted life. For that mistake, I was banished here to Earth."

Silence reigns in the apartment for several heartbeats. "But things haven't been so bad. I basically landed in Cody and Aida's laps, and they took me in without too many questions. They got me here. Personally, I think it was God's consolation prize. He said I was the best Fate they'd ever had. And He didn't relish the idea of banishing me."

I look into Kismet's eyes, desperate to know what she thinks.

"You had dinner with them a while ago," she said. "You said it was a celebration, but not of what. I assumed it was a birthday party for one of the kids or something. But you've been at the shop for just over a year, haven't you?"

"Your memory is astounding," I say, trying to give her a break from puzzling it out. It's not important. What matters is where I am now.

"You were marking the day you fell. The day they found you," she says quietly as she looks past me, putting the last piece of my puzzle into place.

I don't respond to that. I simply hold her hands, waiting for her to decide how she'll handle the truth.

The silence that stretches between us weighs heavily on me, so it's a relief when she finally speaks.

"So you came from heaven?"

"I did."

"And you created me?"

"I did."

"And you were so taken by me that you were ultimately banished to Earth?" She doesn't look at me while she asks these questions. She's absently working a loose thread on her shorts, staring at a spot on the wall.

I follow her gaze. "I was."

"Can you prove any of this?" she asks.

"Maybe. If you need me to."

I watch her breathe slowly in and out as she considers my information.

"And Fia, she's like you, isn't she? She's from the heavens too?"

I hesitate before nodding. "I can't tell you anything else about her. You know she'll have our heads for talking about her behind her back."

Kismet moves on without acknowledging my statement. "And Andrew..." Her voice catches in her throat.

"Yes. Nothing that I said to you in the days after his death was untrue. His death was unfair in every sense of the word. He was supposed to live a long and happy life with you. I don't understand what happened, why his life was cut so short."

"So what can you do now that you're stuck on Earth? Anything?"

I sigh, not sure how much detail I want to give her. "Back home, one of my friends was a Reaper. Michaela was her name. I've been searching for her or one of her friends. Reapers are the only heavenly beings that can go back and forth between Earth and the heavens. Fia seems to think the search is futile, and we should just let her come to us."

She nods as if she understands, but her vacant expression says otherwise. "A Reaper..."

"Reapers help human souls transition to the heavens or to hell, as the case may be."

Her eyes find me again, and I see a hint of fear in them. "You don't think—"

I cut her off before she has to say something terrible out loud. "No, I don't. Andrew is in the heavens, waiting for you." I take her hand in both of mine, stopping her from toying with the thread on her shorts. "And I hope he has to wait a very long time."

She doesn't respond, and silence returns to the tiny apartment. I'm not sure what will happen next. I don't think a bolt of lightning will come down and strike me dead for telling her. But I brace myself for some kind of consequence anyway.

When she speaks again, her voice is soft and hesitant. "Penn, I believe you. I've seen the beauty you can create out of literally nothing. I'll never forget the feeling I experienced when we first met. Like you knew me better than I knew myself. But I couldn't explain why. It was one of the reasons why I nearly told you to get lost. You were creeping me out."

"I'm pretty sure you said as much at the time, but you pretended it was a joke."

She doesn't laugh like I hope she will. But she does keep talking. "But just because I believe you doesn't mean I can get my head around what you're telling me."

With that one sentence, all the wind comes out of my sails, and I slump over. "You're talking about myths and fairy tales being real. I'm not sure I can just nod my head and be one hundred percent okay with that."

Nodding, I ask her, "Would you like me to go?"

"What? No," she says automatically, and then reconsiders. "Maybe. I don't know. I need time to think."

"Okay, I'll go for a walk. Text me in a few hours. If you still need more time, I'll grab a room for the night at the hotel down the street." I stand to go, but she doesn't release my hand.

"You know I love you, right?" she says as her eyes fill with tears, making the green in them shimmer.

"You know I love *you*, right?" She nods and lets me go.

Being mid-August, it's quite warm out, so I just grab my keys and start walking. I head down to the park and sit for a bit, watching the couples wander the quiet paths and feed the birds. I consider calling Fia, but I know what she'll say to me. I got myself into this mess. "You saw that pile of crap, and you stepped in it anyway." I can hear her voice as clearly as if she's standing right here next to me. So I keep walking through the city streets.

Eventually, I find myself back at the cemetery, standing in front of Andrew's gravestone. "Well, my friend. What do I do now?"

Andrew doesn't answer, of course, and I chuckle. "Just like

you to give me judgmental silence. Didn't know you were friends with such a freak, did you?"

I glance at my watch. It's after midnight. Just over three hours since I left. Checking my phone, I see I've still received no word from Kismet, so I text her.

OK to come back?

I walk over to a nearby tree and lean on it while I wait for her response. Some part of me hopes the old tree will give me strength. I wait five more minutes for an answer before I start walking home. It isn't like her not to answer a text, and a sense of dread washes over me, making the distance home feel like a million miles.

Maybe she's in the tub, or she could have already gone to bed. Maybe it's nothing at all to worry about. Still, I quicken my pace until I'm flat out running back to our apartment. I climb the stairs leading over the shop two at a time, only stopping when I reach the upstairs hallway. What I see there staggers me down to my very soul.

Michaela gives me a sad look as she steps out of my apartment. She's holding Kismet's hand.

"No," I whisper. Kismet looks at me, confusion masking her features. She tries to go to me, but Michaela holds her hand tight and tugs her down the hall away from me.

"Michaela, wait! Please. What's happening? Don't take her from me. *Please.* Her thread is longer than this!" I beg, but the two women fade into the dim light at the end of the hall, leaving me alone on Earth.

FOURTEEN

If I thought questions plagued me after Andrew died, I was wrong. In the hours and days after Kismet's death, question after question after question shakes my soul. How did this happen? Why? What could I have done to save her? Is this my punishment for telling her the truth? Or is it part of my banishment? Did someone wish to destroy my life on Earth by snipping short first Andrew's thread and then Kismet's? Or is Webber taking his revenge on me by erasing my two most glorious creations?

There are no answers for my questions, but Webber seems the most likely culprit. I can't imagine the repercussions of taking a soul like Kismet's before her time. If I was banished for a stillborn, I shudder to think of what they might do to Webber.

It's no more than he deserves, I think darkly as I sit with Fia in my apartment above the shop. We don't speak much. She knows my questions. She's heard them all. She's just here with me. I called her after I got home that night, and she hasn't left since.

Cedric steps in again, just as he did when Andrew died. He's the one who calls Kismet's folks; he's the one who makes all the arrangements for her funeral. Cody and Aida drop by daily to make sure I eat at least one meal.

Finally, wanting some time to myself before the funeral, I

convince Fia to go home for a while. Cedric stops by to see me. I'm sitting in the hallway when he arrives, staring at the place where Michaela and Kismet disappeared, willing them to return.

"What are you doing out here?"

I shrug. "Nothing."

"Clearly. Are you locked out?"

I shake my head no.

"Well, I'm hungry. Want to eat?" he asks, holding up a take-out bag from some place up the street.

I shrug again, and Cedric nudges me with his foot. "Come on, man. I'm not about to feed you out in the hall like you're some overgrown toddler. Get up and let's eat." His tone is firm but not harsh. It's just enough to spur me into movement.

"How long were you out there?" Cedric asks.

I shrug a second time as I go through the motions of getting plates and silverware out for dinner. Absently, I get out three place settings. I don't even realize it until we're already seated around the table.

I stare at her empty seat, and Cedric tries to ignore it.

"Did you hear from the hospital yet?" he asks as he gets out the boxes of food.

"Yes, I did. She died of natural causes, just like Andrew did."

"That's odd," Cedric says.

"Yes, it is."

"You weren't here?"

"No. I told you. We had a fight, so I went out for a walk."

"What were you fighting about?" Cedric asks.

I search his face in an effort to read him. He's only looking for answers, the same way I am, but his questions aren't the right ones. "Doesn't much matter now, does it?"

Cedric stabs at his Japanese noodles. "No, I don't suppose it does."

We eat in silence for a while, until Cedric asks another question. "They're doing a memorial service for her on Broadway over the weekend, did you see that?"

I nod. She wasn't on Broadway for long, but everyone there

loved her. They sold out almost every night she was on stage. The community is reeling almost as much from her sudden death as I am.

"Think you'll go?"

"Probably." I push the food around on my plate, thinking about Michaela's sad expression. Why wouldn't she talk to me? Is it because I was banished? Or because there wasn't time for her to explain? She seemed so sad. It was the first time I'd ever seen that look on her face, but then again, it was the first I'd ever seen her in action. It can't be easy to constantly take souls from their loved ones.

"Penn…" Cedric trails off, as if he has something delicate to say. I look up at him in an effort to give the man at least some of my attention. "What will you do?"

I just look at him. What *will* I do? I'm stuck on Earth for an eternity. And now it seems as if I will spend that eternity completely alone.

Rather than let me despair, he offers a solution. "You might want to consider coming back to work. I've seen how you can lose yourself in it. It might help." He takes a bite of food, giving me time to consider. "Not today of course, or tomorrow, but soon. Don't sit around the apartment alone for too long, okay? It isn't good for you."

"Oh, it isn't?" I heatedly say. "How do you know what's good for me?"

"I know that sitting out in the hallway like that isn't good for anyone." Cedric eyes me with a raised eyebrow. "Listen, I'm sorry for everything that's happened to you, but sitting here alone won't change it."

"That's true." What he says gets my wheels turning. My plan to corner Michaela didn't work—not even when I saw her face to face. Maybe it's time to try to find a Watcher. What do I have to lose at this point? Now that Kismet is no longer with me, there's much less of a risk. I have been left with holes filled with questions where my loved ones used to be.

I know Cedric is right; I can't just sit around stewing. But I have to form a plan.

Cedric must see my mind working. "What?"

"I'm just thinking you're right. Sitting here won't get me any answers."

Cedric's eyes narrow as he watches me eat my food in a very utilitarian way. I'm not enjoying it, but I still mechanically bring the food to my face.

I suspect my friend knows there's more to what I've said than I care to elaborate on at the moment, but he doesn't ask, and I don't offer the information.

"I'll come back to work on Monday, okay? I'm sure there's plenty to do," I say, trying to appease Cedric. That will give me the weekend to recover from Kismet's funeral, which is on Friday, the day after tomorrow. Thinking about it turns the food in my mouth bitter, and I forcefully push the plate away.

If Cedric notices, he doesn't comment. "Good. That'll be good." We don't discuss it any further. We just start cleaning up in silence.

"Thank you for bringing dinner," I say as I walk Cedric to the door.

"Of course. I'll see you on Friday. Don't loiter in the hall, okay? I mean it. It's weird."

Rather than respond, I stare down the hall as Cedric pats me on the arm and walks away. Once again, I'm alone.

Friday washes over me like a vat of hot tar. I hold out my hands, trying to stop it, but there's nothing I can do. It consumes me, pouring over my mouth, lungs, and eyes, covering me in blackness.

Her funeral is closed to the public, so only her close friends and family are in attendance. She's buried next to Andrew because I know that's the way she'd want it to be. Now they can spend eternity together. Maybe that's all there is to it. They were fated to be together, and when they couldn't do that on Earth, she naturally followed him into heaven. Maybe her thread was so damaged by Andrew's death that she simply died. Who knows? I'm growing tired of the constant questions, and now they're all for nothing.

Her parents stand on the other side of the grave, her mother a total basket case, as any mother would be, and her dad standing behind her like a cold, stone statue. They don't speak to me as they leave. They never agreed with Kismet's decision to make our relationship romantic, particularly since it seemed to confirm their initial suspicions about us after Andrew died. So she didn't speak with them much this past year, and the last time they saw each other was that horrible night in my apartment. I suspect the regret they both feel might crush them, and I can only hope they won't succumb. I want the domino effect created by Andrew's death to end.

Fia stands with me during the service, holding my hand, holding me up. As people leave, she tries to pull me away, but I'm not ready. I can't go with her.

"All right. Take all the time you need, honey. You know how to reach me when you need me."

Finally, I'm alone at Kismet's side, looking down into the grave at her casket, littered with pink flowers. I hold a single white rose. The distance between us feels so great—so much vaster than when she was on Earth and I was in the heavens. I collapse to the ground, sorrow overwhelming me. It's over. *Truly.* My banishment begins at this moment. Without her, my life is nothing.

After a few moments, I drop my white rose down among the pink ones, and hoist myself up. I start walking, finding myself leaning against the big tree near their graves, the one I leaned against while I was trying to reach Kismet that fateless night. Tears run down my cheeks as I slide down to the ground next to the tree. I lean heavily against it, wanting it to swallow me whole, willing it to take my burdens from me.

What if I'm at fault for her death? What if they really did take her because of what I told her? Or what if she and Andrew both died because of the ripples my appearance caused in their lives? Am I doomed to live out my banishment as some kind of angel of death? Bringing all the lives I touch to an early end? The guilt I feel brings on a new wave of sobs.

Minutes pass, and then hours, but I don't even consider getting up and going home. I can't think past this moment. The black tar so engulfs me, I can't move my arms and legs. I can't leave her there. It's too final. Up until this moment, it was easy to pretend she was just away. That she was at a dress rehearsal, or having drinks with her coworkers. Now I have no choice but to accept that she's truly gone, and the world seems like such a dark, dark place.

"Penn?" I hear a familiar voice softly calling my name.

My breath catches in my throat as I look up.

"Michaela."

FIFTEEN

I can't die, so I'm confused to see her there. I look around, searching for someone she's here to collect. But it's just the two of us. Workers filled in Kismet's grave while I was leaning against the tree. Darkness fell hours ago, and Michaela is standing just beyond Kismet's resting place, barely visible.

Seeing Michaela there, so angelic in her gown that flows white at her shoulders and gradually fades to gray, then black at the bottom, totally concealing her feet, I can't be mad at her for taking Kismet from me. When I finally bring myself to look at her face, her expression banishes what little traces of anger may have been left. Pure and total anguish twists her typically joyful face.

I reach out to Michaela, wanting so badly to connect with this soul who knows my pain firsthand.

But she doesn't move from her spot, so I stop short.

"What are you doing here?" The question comes out a little more accusatory than was intended.

"Something isn't right, Penn. I can't put my finger on what's going on, but…" She trails off, as if she's been searching for the same answers I am.

"I knew it." I breathe.

"Kismet and Andrew aren't the only two who have died

before their time."

I put out a hand and lean on a nearby headstone, needing to stabilize myself from the weight of the news she's heaped on my shoulders. It's happening to others.

"Webber?"

"What about him?"

"I assumed he might be behind it, since Andrew and Kismet were the first to go."

"But they weren't," she says, adamant. "We didn't notice it right away. But it started before you left. That's what I was trying to tell you and your sisters that day. It's happening more and more frequently now. There are names popping up on my list that weren't scheduled to be there for years—decades, in most cases." She nods her head toward Kismet's grave.

"And that poor girl." A tear trickles down Michaela's cheek as she remembers taking the love of my life. "She was so confused and reluctant. She knew it wasn't right. It wasn't her time."

"So it wasn't because I inserted myself into her life? It wasn't because I told her who I was?" I say absently, almost to myself.

"What? No. How could it be? It started before you left. And unless you also told Andrew and a handful of other souls, that can't be the cause."

"No. She was the only one. I had just told her that night. She was overwhelmed, so I went for a walk. That's when you decided to come for her. If I'd been there, I would have tried to stop you." I should feel relieved. But I don't. Something is so wrong with the world right now that it sours what little hope is left in me.

She smiles sadly at me. "Penn, you know you can't stop one of us. Once a name is on our list, that's it."

"Were you the one who came for Andrew?" I ask quietly.

"No. I was on another assignment that day. I'm so sorry, Penn. About everything."

"So it's not Webber? He was my only real suspect," I say as I sit down right there in the middle of the cemetery. She sits next to me Indian-style, wrapping her dress around her knees.

"I don't think so. Although he certainly didn't waste any

time to get comfortable in your spot. Truth be told, even Galenia is having trouble getting along with him. If he's not careful, he won't last."

I frown. "I don't like hearing that. I want the girls to be happy."

"I know. I'm sorry."

We sit in silence for a few moments, and the wind blows Michaela's blonde hair away from her face and off her shoulders. She turns her face to it and closes her eyes. "You know, as hard as my job is sometimes, I really do love it on Earth, especially the wind. It's almost like it carries the breath of those who have passed."

I breathe it in, and it's remarkably fresh for the city. I try to let it energize me, but the week's events have left me so bitterly tired. Leaning forward, I rest my head in my hands. "Michaela, why are you here?"

"I need your help, Penn. I need you to come home."

SIXTEEN

I look up to get a clearer look at her, needing to know if she's serious. But she just looks at me, almost pleading. She's serious.

"Michaela, I was banished. I can't go home. Finding a Reaper or another fallen angel was my best option for getting answers, but it seems like you have just as many questions as I do. I don't see how I can help."

"I do. And I think we can get answers together." She's resolved. Like she hasn't even considered I might push back, that I won't want to help.

"How exactly? I don't think you're listening to me. I can't go home."

"I think I can bring you back with me."

My mouth hangs open as she sucks the rebuttal from me with that one simple phrase. I can travel back with her? "How?" I ask incredulously.

"It would be just like taking a soul as far as I can tell."

I raise an eyebrow at her. "As far as you can tell?"

She shrugs and smiles weakly at me. "I mean, I've never tried to bring a banished Fate back into heaven before. I'm kind of a rule follower, if you know what I mean."

I laugh out loud for the first time in over a week. "Yes, Michaela, I know what you mean." I think about all the times she left our games to get back to work. She's a good girl to the extreme. Her willingness to break the rules this way means that whatever's happening is even worse than I initially thought.

"How bad is it? How many souls?"

"I don't know exactly when it started, so it's hard to know for sure. We know of at least a half a dozen. Kismet is the latest."

"Who are they? Are they all related like Andrew and Kismet were?"

"Not that I can tell," she says.

I think for a moment. Even though his motivation still doesn't make sense, all signs point to Webber. Michaela is just hoping for the best. Who else could be doing it? He is one of the only ones with access to everything he needs to cut lives short.

"What about the tapestry? What is this doing to it?"

"I haven't seen it," she says, a hint of regret in her voice.

"Webber has access to the tapestry, the threads, everything he would need to do this. I'm sorry, I know you think he's innocent, but he has the means."

"But not the motivation," Michaela adds.

I can't argue that. "Do you have any other suggestions?"

"Yes. I suggest we stop guessing so we can get back home and find out what exactly is going on." She stands up, ready to go.

"What about my sisters? Why can't they help you?"

"They are helping me, as much as they can. But they have work to do, just like I do. We need you. Now." She looks down at me, waiting for me to join her.

I think of Fia, Cedric, Aida, and Cody. They will wonder what happened to me. And Cedric. He will not only miss me as a friend; my absence will affect him financially. The shop depends on my skills.

"Michaela, I can't just go. I have ties here."

"When we get back, you can write them a note. I will make sure it gets delivered."

"But Cedric. I'm working in his shop. Things are going really well…"

"He will cope. I'm sure he had the shop long before you started working there, and he'll have it long after. This is bigger than all of them, Penn."

She is giving me a purpose, something I desperately need, so I rise and brush the grass from my suit. As I do so, I remember why I was in this cemetery in the first place. I look back at my beloved's grave, sick with the knowledge that this is the last moment we will share, ever. I won't be reunited with her in the heavens. I will never see her again. I turn back to Michaela, and the pain I feel is mirrored on her face.

"Go say goodbye, Penn," she urges.

I walk slowly over to Kismet, recently covered over with dirt, not knowing what to say. I always knew this day would come, but I thought there would have been more time to prepare, more time for us to make memories together.

Looking down at her, I'm not sure of anything anymore. The workers have placed one of the floral arrangements on top of her grave, and it stands out against the dirt, sparkling with dew, just like she did in her life. I know she'll be just as much of a star in heaven. And she'll be with Andrew. I try to take comfort in that.

"Kismet, I have work to do now. I'm sorry I couldn't save you, but I hope with all my heart that you are happy now." As I turn and walk away, I feel sluggish. Like the act of saying goodbye has added more weight to my burdens instead of lessening them.

"I shouldn't have to say goodbye. Not yet," I say to Michaela.

She takes my hand, touching me for the first time that night "I know. That's why we have to go home."

As soon as she takes my hand, I feel myself fading. Without really intending to, I struggle to stay, to hold on to the Earth, to be with Kismet. But Michaela won't let me.

"I'm used to dealing with people who want to stay, but I didn't expect to have to encourage you."

"I know." I look over my shoulder at Kismet one last time. "I don't want to leave her."

"If it helps, she isn't there anymore. Right now, she's probably getting pampered as the newest surprise arrival in heaven. She knows no sorrow anymore, Penn. That's what you always wanted for her."

I nod and put one foot in front of the other as we walk. She's right. Trying to gain some strength from that single truth, I turn forward and head back home.

———

The journey is odd for me. My fall was an assault on the senses, all rushing wind leading to a jarring fall. However, the walk home is so much more peaceful.

The Earth fades away, replaced by billowing white clouds, although it doesn't feel like we're climbing. Rather, it seems like a thick fog has simply descended upon us. If it weren't so quiet, I would've thought we were still walking around the city.

"Normally, this is where the soul I'm guiding watches their favorite memories—birthdays, graduations, weddings, babies, all the wonderful things about life—at least for the happy souls. And all the things that made them, them. But you're not a human, so apparently, we don't get to watch anything."

I chuckle, but the sound quickly fades in the cloudy space. "So, what's your favorite memory that you've ever seen?"

"Oh gosh. There are so many. Grandparents holding their grandbabies for the first time. Little kids getting puppies. But I think my favorite was one of an old man. I'd taken his wife years before, but I didn't remember the two were connected until I saw her in his memories. They weren't without their flaws. Once or twice, they'd almost broken up. Which is why I was surprised when we came to his last memory, the one we experienced before we arrive at the gates. It's usually the most defining moment of the soul's life. His wasn't their wedding day, the day she died, or any of those important days in between. It was nothing. A day after one of their worst arguments. Someone said the word divorce in that fight; it was their lowest moment.

"But just a day later, they were sitting on a bench together looking out at the lake. Neither of them spoke. They just stared out at the water. Each was wondering what they'd done, if their choices had been wrong, if they'd made too many mistakes to ever make it right again. And then something magical happened.

"While they both looked out over the water, the man reached out his hand and put it on the bench, in the middle of the space between them. For a moment, the wife acted like she didn't notice, but I saw the slight change in her posture, the way she sat up a little straighter at his movement. But she didn't let him sit there with his hand out for long. Without looking at him, she put her hand on his, and they sat there, holding hands, watching the ducks swim past. And it was in that moment he knew they were going to make it, and that no choices that led him to her could ever be wrong."

I smile as we walk through the fog, thinking how sometimes life's greatest moments can be the small ones.

"What was your favorite memory so far?" Michaela asks me.

"On Earth?"

"Any time, I suppose."

"You know, I'd have to say, more than creating Kismet and Andrew, it was getting to see them meet. It was such a magical moment to see two souls that were perfectly suited for each other find their other halves. In that moment, I felt like my banishment had been worth it." Perhaps it's odd that this moment is more special to me than the time she and I spent together on Earth. But the more I think about it, the more I realize she was never really mine. The moment I made Andrew, I set her free. And together, they were beautiful.

"You introduced them, right?"

"I did. Yes."

"When were they supposed to meet before you fell?"

I shudder at this reminder of one of my greatest fears. The ripples caused by my presence. Did I intervene too much? "Do you think that's what set this in motion for Kismet and Andrew?

Do you think I tampered too much with their fates?" A part of me realizes it doesn't make much sense. If nothing else, it doesn't explain the others who were taken before their time, but horror builds in my stomach anyway. My breath comes in short gasps.

Michaela squeezes my hand as we walk. "No. I don't think you tampered too much. They would've met without you. They were meant to be together. I just wondered how soon, that's all. I didn't mean to cause you pain." She hangs her head as she walks, as if she's failed me in some way.

I look over at her and nod. "You're right. They would've met anyway. And it would've been soon. It's just hard not to have answers. I am a Fate. I'm supposed to know everything."

She smiles as the fog starts to clear. "We're almost there," she says, and I stop walking.

"What are we going to do when we get there? I can't be seen. And you can't be seen with me, or you'll end up banished right along with me for harboring a fugitive."

"I know. I'm just trusting this will be okay."

"I'm thinking that's not the best plan."

"Listen, not a lot of people wander around the gates. There's a good chance we can get to my quarters without being seen."

"Your quarters?"

"Well, you can't go to yours." She says it so matter-of-factly. Like I should know why I can't go there. But I don't. She has to elaborate. "Webber is staying in them. They're his quarters now."

That statement hits me like a freight train. Of course Webber is staying in my quarters. He's the Spinner now.

"I'm sorry," she says quietly as we stand there in the dwindling fog.

I nod. "I don't know what I was thinking."

"Anyway, you can't be seen wandering around. If you're caught, you'll find yourself wishing for your banishment. They will eliminate you. Completely."

We've all heard the horror stories, but it ratchets my blood pressure up a few levels to hear it out loud.

"You'll have to be careful about where you go and who you

ask for information."

"Who *I* ask?"

She nods. "Yes, well, my workload has gotten a bit intense lately, with all the unexpected deaths. I'll help you in any way I can, but I can't make any promises."

"How am I supposed to ask people what's going on without being seen?"

She shakes her head, knowing she's asking the impossible. "I didn't say it would be easy."

I nod and look down at our clasped hands as we stand in the mist facing each other. She came and rescued me, putting her whole existence on the line to bring me home. Occasionally a slight breeze that comes from nowhere ruffles her hair or the bottom of her dress.

"Thank you, Michaela. You have saved me, in every possible way."

Without letting go of my hand, she throws herself at me and pulls me into a tight hug. I try to let go of her hand, to embrace her with both hands, but she holds fast. "Don't let go," she commands. Instinctually, I listen.

"We're so close. If you let go of me, you'll be lost. The humans who let go of their Reapers become ghosts, wandering the Earth forever."

I pull back a little to look at her. "How many have you lost?"

"Three." She's quiet for a moment as I hold her. "One was a child who didn't understand. That was the worst one. She wanted to go back to her mommy. And she did. She haunted that poor woman for the rest of her life. It was horrible when I had to come back and take her, leaving her child alone on Earth."

She takes a deep, shuddering breath. "But we shouldn't talk about such dark things as we approach the gates, or we'll end up at the wrong one."

"What?" I ask.

"That's how I know where to bring the soul. If their final memory is something... unsavory, I know they're destined for hell, and that's the gate that will appear at the end of the road. Then I know to prepare myself for a fight. But there are guards at that gate that usually help. They're trained for that kind of thing. All I have to do is get them there. I rarely go through them."

I nod, shuddering at the thought of the guardians of hell. I hope I never have to see them myself.

"Which gate do you anticipate for me?" I ask, not sure what to expect.

"Neither, really, since you're not human. I'm hoping the gate home will appear, and we can just go on through."

"What if the gate of hell appears?" I ask nervously as I hold fast to my friend.

She pushes back a little and looks up. "If that happens, I will let you go. I don't know what will happen to you, but I won't let you spend eternity in hell."

I nod, trying to take assurance in that thought.

Finally, she backs away from me, still holding fast to my hand, and we stand next to each other for a few moments. "Are you ready?"

"As ready as I'll ever be."

She smiles at me in what I interpret as an attempt at reassurance, so I squeeze her hand as we walk together through the mists.

When the mist finally disappears, we stand in front of three gates. The one on the left is white, the one on the right is black, and the one in the middle is gold.

"Huh. It's weird to stand in front of all three at the same time. Normally, the only one that appears is the one intended for the soul, and then ours will appear once I've delivered them." She stands in awe of them for a few minutes, and they truly are beautiful to behold.

They aren't simply white, gold, and black. They are intricately carved with detailed representations of what is held within. I look down at Michaela's hand, and she nods, indicating it's okay to venture forth on my own now that we're free of the mist. I let her go and wander to the white gate first.

It tells a story, I realize. Adam and Eve are at the bottom. Working my way up, I see Cain and Abel, and eventually Noah, Abraham, Isaac, Jacob, Moses, and Jesus. But Jesus is only at the halfway point. There are many others above Him whom I don't recognize.

"Who are all these people?" There are men, women, and children climbing toward the top of the gate, all of them reaching outstretched arms to the heavens.

"Most of them haven't been born yet. But they will all play some vital role in the history of humanity."

I move toward the gold door, carved with angels, Reapers, and human-like figures clasping hands. There are Keepers standing in front of stacks and stacks of books, Weavers working on the great tapestry of life, and finally the Fates, standing around the cauldron. All three of them are women.

"This was made some years ago. Long before you became a Fate," Michaela says, as if apologizing for the oversight.

But I don't see it that way. My heritage is carved into that gate. I come from a long line of women, and it's nothing to be ashamed of. It's something I embrace.

I reach out for the gate, wanting to touch the sisters of my heritage, but Michaela stays my arm. "Don't touch it until you're ready to go in."

The only gate left is the great black gate. Part of me doesn't even want to go over to it, and I let my hand hover over the three sisters as I give it a closer look. Although it's the same size as the other two, it seems bigger, more imposing, and a thousand times less inviting.

Still, my curiosity gets the best of me, and I cautiously approach the gate, taking care to keep my hands clasped behind my back, lest I touch the gate by mistake.

But I don't find what I expect. I think demons and other creatures of nightmares will be carved there. But instead, the gate tells a sad tale of humans who have gone astray, and been forever parted from their loved ones. Every single human carved on it is crying. It overwhelms me. I take a step back, but the further I back up, the bigger the gate seems to get as it looms over me.

Eventually, I bump into Michaela. "It's okay," she says. "I know it can be a bit… overwhelming." She puts her hands on my shoulders, trying to steady me, but my heart is racing, and I have a hard time tearing my eyes away from the depictions on the gate.

"Isn't there any chance for redemption for those trapped behind those gates?"

"They had many chances for redemption before they landed here." She says it without emotion, as if that's the way it is. I suppose for her, it is. Her tone reminds me of the ICU nurse I met—guarded, not jaded. If she didn't take a very unemotional approach to the gates, being a Reaper would be a very difficult job indeed.

Without anything left to explore, we both turn to face the gold gate.

"I guess there's nothing left to do but go inside," I say.

"One last thing."

She lingers in the cloudy area next to the base of the gate. Reaching a hand into the clouds, she pulls out a pile of hidden clothing.

It's robes and sandals in heavenly style. "If you go in wearing that, they'll mistake you for a human and flip out."

But they aren't Spinner's robes. I hold them up for a better look. Spinner's colors are a shimmering light gold color. But these are tan, with a brown belt at the center. "A Keeper?"

"No one looks at the Keepers. They keep to themselves unless approached for information. Let's just hope no one does that to you. If you keep your head down and your hood up, with a little bit of luck, you won't get caught."

"If I do…" I hesitate, looking deep into Michaela's blue eyes, silently thanking her for everything.

"If you do, I won't even know about it. You'll just disappear without so much as a goodbye. And I won't even be able to ask about you. So don't get caught. I don't want to worry about you for the rest of eternity."

"You wouldn't have to. I'd be gone."

"Exactly."

I take the robes from her and change. Once I'm done, I leave my human clothes carefully concealed behind the cloud. "If anyone should find them, we're toast," I say.

"They won't. These have been hidden for almost a week on Earth. As soon as Kismet's name appeared on my list, I knew I had to come get you. I just needed to wait for the right time."

I think of my last moments by her graveside. "I couldn't have left her before today anyway."

Michaela nods knowingly as we approach the gold gate. "You go in first, I'll be right behind you. Don't call attention to yourself. No one can know you're here."

"That's going to make it hard to do any kind of recon work."

"We'll talk about it more later." She gives me a little shove toward the gate, and I put my hand out. The moment I make contact, the gate dissolves and I pass through it.

I expect a bustle of activity, but I'm not sure why. I've never even been to this side of the heavens before, and I've never seen the gates from either side. And based on how empty it appears to be, I imagine not too many others have seen it either.

Michaela bumps into me in the doorway. "Sorry, I expected you to keep moving," she says. "Only Reapers frequent this area. If one of them sees you, they might think it's odd, but you probably won't be questioned. We're all too busy lately to pay much attention to anything but our work."

That's a little sad. "Don't you want a break?"

Michaela looks at me like I have six heads, but then she actually pauses to consider my question. "Maybe. But to even have a chance at getting a break, I need help. That's where you come in."

I nod, doing my best to keep my head down and my face concealed as we walk. Because of that, I can't get a good sense of where we're going. Michaela guides me with a light touch on my elbow, telling me when to turn, when to slow down, and when to speed up.

I occasionally hear other footsteps, but the Reapers—if that's what they are—never speak to us. All I can do is hope they won't notice the banished soul walking among them.

A few twists and turns later, we arrive at a door. Michaela ushers me inside and shuts it behind her.

"Okay, you should be safe in here."

I pull the hood off and look around. It's much different from my quarters. Hers doesn't look out on the heavens like mine did. Mesmerized, I walk to her back wall, with my hand held out. "Earth," I breathe.

"Yes. Reapers get to see anything on Earth they'd like. I change mine based on my mood. That's a waterfall in the Brazilian rainforest. One of my favorites. I haven't gotten to see it in real life yet, but it's on my list. But I have seen some other beautiful things."

In an instant, the wall changes to the painted deserts of Arizona, then to the northern lights in Alaska, to the colorful fish of the Great Barrier Reef, to a volcano in Hawaii, to a lightning storm, and on and on as I watch all the beauty I missed with my mouth hanging open.

"I thought New York was nice," I whisper, not wanting to disturb the moment.

She giggles. "It *is* nice. They have some great things. But the world is more than that. So much more," she says. There's an undeniable hint of longing in her voice.

I understand. Now that I'm home, I wonder if I'll ever be able to go back and see all the things Michaela has seen. Although part of me is glad to be back in the heavens among my friends, a larger part of me misses Earth, and my family there. The feeling makes me feel out of sorts, as if I don't know which place is truly my home.

Michaela doesn't give me much time to dwell. "I have to go. I've already been gone too long. I can't let them notice. I'll be back when I can. Try to discover what you can, but for the love of God—"

I cut her off. "Don't get caught." I nod. "I know."

"Good luck," she says.

"You too. I hope you don't get any more surprise names on your list."

"Me too," she says. And with that, she leaves me alone in her room.

I look around the small space, similarly furnished to my own. I never thought I would find myself back in these surroundings again, and now that I'm here—as a fugitive—I'm not sure what to do.

First thing's first. I need to write a note to Fia so she can tell the others I'm okay, which is true—for now. There is no need for everyone to know the danger I'm in.

Fia,

Thank you so much. For everything. I hope you know how much you mean to me.

I've gone home. You were right, and so was I. Michaela needs my help, so I've gone back to the heavens with her. Something isn't right, and Andrew and Kismet aren't the only ones to have been taken before their time.

Please tell Cedric I'm sorry. And tell the others I'm all right, and I love them. I'll check in on you all from time to time, and maybe someday I can come back.

I will make this right, or die trying, Fia.

—Penn

I fold the letter and leave it out for Michaela. Next up is to find some answers. But as I sink down into a chair facing a wide expanse of turquoise water and white sand beach, I wonder where in the heavens I'm going to start.

SEVENTEEN

Because I'm dressed as a Keeper, my first thought is to go to their side of heaven and search for anomalies among their literature. It's quiet work, where no one will bother me. But I fear it will take too long, *if* the information I need is even in there.

So I decide to poke around where I am. Maybe if I can see the names for myself, I can make a connection between them. It would be easier with Michaela's help, but she isn't back yet. Probably still trying to make up for the time she lost while she was collecting me.

With absolutely no idea of where to go, I set out, hoping to find what I need before someone finds me.

As I wander the halls of the Reapers, I find myself wishing I'd followed Michaela when she left, so I would at least know my way around a little.

"Keeper," a deep voice calls.

I freeze. I don't recognize the voice, but if the soul behind it recognizes me, I'm done. Briefly, I consider running, but I know I won't get far. My best chance is to play it cool and make the guy believe I'm a Keeper.

"Yes?" I ask as I turn to face the owner of the booming voice.

A tall, muscular man with dark skin, dark hair, and dark eyes, he's dressed in a black shirt and pants that fade from black to gray to white. A Reaper. But he isn't familiar to me. I can only hope he doesn't recognize me either.

"Are you lost?"

I clear my throat. "Yes, actually. I'm looking for the most recent list of names. For our records."

"Of course. This way." He holds out his arm and falls into step beside me as we walk in that direction.

"Are you new? I've never known the Keepers to send someone to collect the names before."

"Yes, I'm new."

"I see." He chuckles to himself. "Are they punishing you for something, or do they really want the names that bad? Usually we deliver them at the end of the day."

"Considering the number of names we've been getting lately, we wanted to get a head start on the task."

The man nods grimly. "There has been a slight influx."

He stops in front of a glass door that pulls silently into the wall, allowing us passage. Inside, LED screens line three walls of the huge room. Names cover the screens, and more than once, I see the list trickle downward so a new name can appear on top.

Pearl Hughes
Frederico Gillam
Jeff Rummel

They're my creations.

Thinking I might take a chance, I ask, "How many surprises have popped up today?"

The man lets out a sharp sigh, but I'm not sure what it's directed at. Me? The situation? The fact that I know about the situation? All three? Despite his obvious hesitation, the man answers. "The last one was about four hours ago. Kismet something."

Four hours ago. It had been just over a week for me.

"Do you have a list of the surprises?" The man gives me a

sidelong look, and I worry I've gone too far. The longer I stay with this man, the greater the chance he will recognize me or realize I'm not a Keeper. I quickly try to cover my tracks. "We're keeping a record of what's happening."

The man nods. "This way."

I follow him to the end of the room, and then over to the corner on the right. There's a door there I couldn't see from where we entered. The door is glass, like all the rest in the Reapers' section of heaven, but this door is an opaque white, so I can't see through it. It blends in seamlessly with the walls. In fact, if the Reaper hadn't led me here, I never would've seen it.

The man leads me to the end of the dark room. A small LED screen is there, with just over half a dozen names on it. Kismet's is among them, as is Andrew's. I know who all of them are. I created each of them.

"I'll leave you now," the man says. "Please, show yourself out."

"Of course. Thank you for your kindness."

The man tilts his head in acknowledgment and leaves. I move some boxes off a chair and take a seat in front of the list, wishing I'd brought something with me to write the names on. Even so, I can tell that Michaela was right—the only two that appear to be related are Andrew and Kismet.

The only fact they have in common is that they are all adults. No children are on the list. That seems odd. There also aren't any elderly people. They're all in their twenties or early thirties. There are only seven of them.

I look at the very first name, the one who started it all. *Nysa Amberry*. What's special about her? She was only twenty-four when she passed, so I must have spun her thread fairly recently. I try to think back to her order, wishing I could touch her hand to get a better picture. She was energetic. I remember that. Energetic but disciplined. A nurse. That's right. The order was for a Healer on Earth. I smile to myself as I put the pieces together, but they still don't add up to a full picture.

As I try to puzzle it out, Michaela comes into the room. "Thought I might find you here when you weren't in my room.

How did you get here?"

"A very kind Reaper helped me out," I say. "Hey, what happened with Nysa?" I nod to her name at the top of the list.

Michaela sighs. "She was the first, we think. An anomaly, or so we hoped. Her death was blamed on some infectious disease she came into contact with in the hospital where she worked. It killed her quickly and quietly, leaving no trace behind, or so the humans said. We Reapers knew something else had happened to her, but we couldn't figure it out."

"What happened when you took her?" I ask.

Michaela scans the room before she speaks. She's obviously nervous talking about it, no matter how private the creepy room appears to be. "She wasn't ready. Just like all the others, her soul knew it wasn't the right time. She didn't have a family yet or anything like that, but she just knew. She fought me some, but quickly gave up when she realized it was futile."

I frown. It's a familiar story, but it doesn't provide us with any information about the who, the why, or the how. I need to spend some time at the tapestry and find a connection between these people. We're missing something.

Michaela glances around again. "We need to get out of here. Someone is going to notice you lingering." I suddenly notice her expression. She seems agitated and flustered.

"You okay?" I ask as we walk back toward her room.

"Just frustrated. And antsy."

I nod, but something nags at me. "This is going to sound horribly insensitive, but there are only seven names on the extra list. How many Reapers do you work with? Why would seven souls make so much more work for you?"

She sighs, and I immediately regret the question. But I want to know. How did they even notice seven names? Seven souls must seem like a drop in the ocean of souls who leave the world each day.

"There are about twenty Reapers total, give or take. The problem is that we were already busy. It's the life of a Reaper. It doesn't help that one of the Reapers is on leave right now. When you consider how many people die each day, and how many of us there are, it's a tremendous workload. So, when one person gets added to a Reaper's list, it dominoes, because it means someone else has to pick up one or two names from our list, then someone else has to pick up a few names from their list, but then another name pops up on someone else's list, and before long, we've lost control of the situation.

"Like I said, a lot of people come easily, not everyone, of course, but it helps the job go faster. When you have a surprise pop up, you know it's going to take longer. You saw the way Kismet looked back at you. She was so confused."

"On top of that, it's happened in just over a week. Nearly one a day. It's exhausting."

We walk in silence for a few minutes as we continue on toward Michaela's quarters.

"I didn't see an obvious connection between the names either. I want to spend some time at the tapestry, see their lives. Maybe I can find something there."

She turns to me in the doorway of her quarters. "Are you crazy? You can't go back there. You'll be recognized. What if Webber is the one who finds you? That'll be it."

"But we need to watch the threads. It's our best chance of finding out what happened," I argue.

"There must be another way." She says it as if that closes the discussion, not giving me the opportunity to respond. Looking back and forth, she makes sure no one sees me go inside. When she's satisfied, she shuts the door behind her.

"You need to be careful coming and going. Someone will think we're having an affair."

I smile. Affairs in the heavens are rare, and those who participate in them are thought to be too much like humans and totally out of touch. "If only that were the least of our concerns."

Her smile manages to banish some of the frustration etching deep lines on her face. It spurs me on.

"Can you imagine the gossip in the common room? The whispers? A Reaper and a Keeper?" I put my hand over my mouth and gasp. "Oh dear."

She slaps at me. "It's only funny because it's true. It really would create quite a scandal. I don't know why, though. Keepers are truly interesting souls."

"Oh, imagine what they'd think if they discovered your lover wasn't a Keeper at all. The speculation that would create! Certainly, they would all decide he was an archangel in disguise, because that's the type of man you deserve."

She wrinkles up her nose. "What do you mean by that? They're so serious."

I look at her, surprised. "The archangels are the best of us," I say simply.

Her smile warms her whole face this time. "That's very kind of you, Penn." Then her expression turns mischievous. "But the angels are too stiff. You saw them. Not exactly the best conversationalists."

"Maybe not. I assumed they were just like that because I was around. Maybe they crack each other up?" I lower my voice, making my best attempt at being serious. "Did you hear the one about the angel who tripped over his wings? No? That's because he fell. Har-har-har."

She shakes her head, but she's still smiling. "All right. We should at least attempt to be constructive."

"I did notice one thing about the list," I say. I'd been stewing over it on the way back to her quarters.

"What?" she asks.

"I don't think Webber would know who the others are. The other five. I mean, he wove them into the tapestry and everything, but why them? Remember how he said he liked the dark threads? There were dark threads in the mix. Why would he cut dark threads short if he likes them? Something doesn't add up."

"I know you're focusing on Webber because he wronged you, but I don't think he's behind this. I truly don't."

"You are too trusting," I accuse.

"Thank you." Her response gives me pause. I didn't mean it as a compliment, but she chose to take it that way, robbing the sting from the barb completely. Honestly, I'm glad. Her kind heart is one of the things I like best about her.

Flashing a small smile at her, I sit down in the nearest chair.

She sees the note I left. "You know what, I'm going to go deliver this while I have a break."

"All work and no play makes Michaela a—"

She cuts me off. "A Reaper. That's what it makes me."

"I know, but take a breath, maybe stop by the observatory to center a bit before diving back in."

She sighs, nods, and her eyes narrow. "Don't do anything stupid while I'm gone."

"We've had this discussion already today."

"I know. Doesn't make it any less true."

I know I'm heading to the weaving room as soon as she's gone, whether she thinks it's a good idea or not. Fates are the only ones who can watch the threads. To others, the tapestry looks like the gorgeous landscape it is, nothing more, nothing less. Because of that, I can't send her to do it. It has to be me.

I nod toward the letter in her hand. "Thank you."

She smiles and walks out, but I'm not far behind her. We both have things to do.

After the day's wanderings, I've learned my way around the Reaper's area enough to make my way out of it. Like all the other factions, it dumps out into the common room. From there, I know how to make my way to my old stomping grounds. Even with my hood concealing some of my peripheral vision, I know exactly where to go. I'm home.

By the time I wander past the workroom where I've spent such a large portion of my life, everyone has gone to bed. I'm glad. I'm not sure I would have possessed the strength to walk past Galenia and Horatia. Plus, I know I can't examine the tapestry during the day. I need time alone with it.

I shut the door behind me and approach the tapestry slowly, taking in its beauty, almost as if I'm seeing it for the first time. I feel so torn between two worlds. A part of me feels like Earth is now my rightful home, but here, seeing the tapestry, I feel the tug of my calling strongly enough that my fingers start to twitch.

From a distance, the tapestry appears undamaged. However, I notice there have been very few new additions since my departure, which means production is way down. I've been gone for over a year on Earth. There should be a whole new section, at least a million threads added. But there's only maybe half that amount. The cascading impact will be tremendous.

I shake my head as I examine the threads. There are so many, it seems an impossible task to find seven specific ones among the billions that make up it up. When we watch threads, we choose them at random, never searching for any one in particular. Kismet's thread was an exception. Between the sparkling gem it was, and the way I'm drawn to it, it's always easy to find. Others though… I'm not sure it's even possible. But I have to try.

Kismet's thread is the easiest to find, so I begin there. I frown as I bring my hand closer to the delicate fabric in front of me. None of the threads around hers are damaged, but a clean cut has been made through her thread. The bottom portion of her thread is missing.

My pulse quickens as my mind races with the possibilities. What would someone want with a portion of her thread? Andrew's thread is next. To my dismay, I discover the same thing. It takes a little more time, but I find the five other threads too, all of them cut short. I notice some damage around the other threads. Nysa was the first, I remember. There are at least three threads around hers that have been shredded and frayed. Those lives will be permanently altered. I look back to Kismet's thread, confirming the lack of damage around hers. It's almost like whoever is doing it is getting better at it with time and practice.

What could it possibly mean?

Settling in, I decide to watch Nysa's thread first. Her life is just as it should be. Until it isn't. The end is just as abrupt and confusing as Michaela described it.

Nysa was a nurse in the oncology ward of a pediatric hospital. It was taxing work, but she found it very rewarding. Her last patient before she passed away was a young boy named Shiloh.

Nysa knew he wouldn't make it. It was a miracle he'd survived as long as he had. His mother seemed very distraught, but the boy seemed to be at peace with his fate.

She tried to comfort the woman out in the hallway. "Shiloh needs you to be strong now."

The woman's tearful expression turned cold. "I don't need you to tell me what I need to be or do right now. My son is dying. I need to save him. Whether you plan on helping me or not."

Nysa straightened, apologized, and excused herself. This was probably the type of thing she had to deal with all too often in her line of work. The rest of her day was filled with paperwork, tending other patients, nothing remarkable. She started to feel ill near the end of the day, and the very next day, she was gone.

That's it. I sit back, sighing. Kismet passed away so quickly, with no signs of illness. Why did Nysa's death take so long? A chill runs down my spine as I examine her damaged thread again. Was her death drawn out because whoever did this didn't make a clean cut?

"Can I help you?"

The familiar voice stops my train of thought cold.

"Hey, don't touch that. Keepers shouldn't touch the tapestry. You might damage it." Webber runs over and grabs my arm, turning me to face him.

EIGHTEEN

The look on Webber's face transforms from surprise to fear as he tries to comprehend what my presence could possibly mean. He drops my arm like a hot potato.

"What are *you* doing here?"

"Maybe I should ask you the same thing," I respond. "Come to take another thread for yourself?"

"What?" Webber takes a step back, glancing around nervously.

His attitude seems to confirm he's the one responsible. He has to be. Otherwise, why would he be so nervous?

"What are you doing with them? I know why you took Andrew and Kismet, but why the others? Why not start with Andrew? Did you need practice to get it right?"

Instead of answering, Webber takes another step back.

I advance on him, taking advantage of my upper hand. "Webber, answer me. Why?"

"I..." he stammers. "I don't know what you're talking about. Don't hurt me."

"What? Why would I hurt you? What have you done to deserve being hurt?"

"Nothing! I swear." He holds up his hands in defense. I'm getting more and more confused. Heavenly beings don't raise their hands against each other. What is Webber so scared of and why?

"Webber, why do you think I'd hurt you? If anything, I would take you to the archangels and report your crimes. But I would never strike you in any way. No matter what you might deserve."

"You are fallen. You don't have to adhere to the rules of heaven anymore."

That gives me pause. Am I forever tainted by my banishment? Is everyone going to be afraid of me? Michaela isn't. "You're an idiot. If you knew me at all, you'd know I wasn't going to hurt you. Now tell me what's going on."

"What are you doing here then?" Webber asks, ignoring my demand. I'm not sure he even heard it. His eyes dart wildly between the tapestry, the door, and me.

"I'm trying to figure out why people are dying before their time on Earth is up. And I have a feeling you're behind it, since Andrew and Kismet were two of the victims."

"What?" he says, genuine horror in his voice. My eyes narrow. Either he's a remarkable actor, or he truly isn't involved. I know Webber. He isn't smart enough for this level of manipulation. But accepting that means accepting the fact that he isn't responsible, and I'm not ready to do that.

"People are dying on Earth, Webber. Well before they were meant to."

Webber's eyes shoot to the tapestry. "I noticed the damage early last week. And then your beautiful thread was cut and removed yesterday," he says, his voice quiet as he cautiously approaches the tapestry, taking care to glance at me on occasion.

Have I really been sitting here looking at the tapestry for that long? When I first arrived in the heavens, Kismet had only just been taken. I shake my head, cursing myself for losing track of time.

"I don't understand it," he adds as he examines the fabric.

"You did this. You had to. You did it to get one final dig in at me." Even as I say it, I know it's not true, but that means we don't have any leads. It means we're stuck.

Webber sinks down into a nearby stool. "*You* got the final dig, Penn," he says quietly.

"I… what?" I ask, growing more and more confused.

"Turns out I'm a much better Weaver than I am a Spinner. I guess I should've known that. Production is the worst it's been in centuries. All because of me. I'm going to be demoted. They just have to find a replacement."

I'm about to speak, to ask more questions, but he sighs and cuts me off before I even get my mouth open. "For God's sake, Penn, I didn't do this," Webber says, his fear totally gone. This is more like the Webber I knew. Impatient. Brash.

"With that kind of sass, you must not be afraid of me anymore," I say, pulling a stool up to the tapestry and taking a seat beside Webber.

"I've just never seen someone who's fallen return. They say the fallen become horrible, twisted version of themselves. Lawless and ruthless."

I laugh, the sound genuine. "Think about that for a moment. Would God really unleash someone like that on His creations on purpose?" In all honesty, it's me who should be afraid of Webber. Of all the people who could have found me here, Webber is the worst. He would do anything to destroy me. Maybe if I can hold on to some of that basic fear, I can convince him to keep his mouth shut.

"No, I suppose not."

We stare at each other for a few moments, each waiting for the other to make a move. But neither of us knows what to do.

"I'm sorry things didn't work out for you," I say.

Webber nods. "Ditto, actually."

I nod. "So you truly don't know what's happening here? I mean, I'm fallen. I could shoot lasers out of my eyes at you to get you to tell me the truth."

Finally, Webber chuckles. The sound doesn't irk me as much as it did in another life. Maybe Webber's right. Falling has changed me some, but not for the worse. It has only made me appreciate the things I left behind. Perhaps even this man I never cared for is not all bad.

"Penn, now who's being stupid? Don't you remember that it's nearly impossible for heavenly beings to lie?"

It hits me like a freight train. I sag down on the stool as the truth barrels down on me. "You're right," I breathe.

Webber reaches out to offer a steadying hand. "You okay?"

"No. I have no idea what's going on. And I need answers. We have to stop this."

Webber nods.

"Did you tell Michaela what you discovered?" I ask.

"No. Everything was already so messed up because of me. I was afraid this was my fault too."

I frown at him. "Webber, it's time to grow a pair. Your information may have helped Michaela. She came to get me to help her. More names keep popping up on her list of souls, more people who are dying before their time. You could've at least tried to stop this, and you didn't." I'm beginning to remember why I didn't care for Webber.

"Look, I'm sorry. It's been a tough time since you left. For everyone."

I narrow my eyes. "What do you mean by that?" Instinct tells me Webber is talking about his sisters, *my* sisters.

"Horatia and Galenia haven't been very happy." He pauses. "One of my first assignments was for a man, or at least I thought it was supposed to be a man. Adventurous and innocent, those were the instructions. But Horatia cut the thread so short, and Galenia gave him some mysterious skin disease. He never grew to be a man. She killed a *kid*. I think they did it to gang up on me. They don't like me much."

I bristle. "You don't know them very well at all, do you? They would never punish a human for something you did, let alone a child. Sometimes kids get sick, but you have to see the larger purpose. Maybe that child will serve as an inspiration to millions of people to find a cure. You can't be a Fate without seeing the bigger picture, Webber. If you don't understand that, it's no wonder you're not doing well." It's harsh, but I can't listen to him accuse my sisters of that. "They're your sisters. Treat them with some respect, man."

Webber looks up at me with a sadness I hadn't noticed before. "No, they're *your* sisters."

I sigh, not knowing what to say to that. I can't bring myself to feel guilty for his downfall. He got what he wanted. It's not my fault he can't handle it. "I'm sorry to hear that they aren't happy. Is that all?"

"Well, I guess so. That, on top of everything else, has made for an unpleasant work environment. I mean, how was I supposed to succeed when you were this rock star Fate?" He points accusingly at me.

"Look, you got what you wanted. Whether you're involved in the major screw up that's going on or not, I'm here to fix it. So you can either quit whining and help me or you can keep your damned mouth shut."

Webber freezes. Heavenly bodies never throw the word "damned" around like that. *Ever.* It hits too close to home, with the city of the damned so nearby. I hold my ground as Webber processes what I said.

"What do you mean by keep my mouth shut?" He deliberately leaves out the damned part.

I kick myself internally for my slip up and watch as Webber's mind chews on what I said.

"If I reveal you, they'll erase you from existence."

"But you're not going to do that, are you." It's a statement, not a question.

A glint shines in Webber's eye, just like the one I saw there when I was being escorted out of heaven.

"Webber, there are too many lives at stake here."

"Too many? Seven people have died. Out of billions. Seven. This is barely a problem. You only care because your beloved Kismet was one of them."

"That may be why it came to my attention, but—"

Webber cuts me off. "Oh, please. Your whole good-guy bit only goes so far with me."

"And your pathetic loser bit only goes so far with me. As you said, I am fallen. I have nothing to lose. And if you threaten me again, I will silence you."

"You said you wouldn't hurt me," Webber says, his tone revealing the tiniest shred of doubt.

"That was before. Now that you're trying to erase me from existence, I may rethink things."

Webber swallows and eyes me warily. Eventually, after letting several tense heartbeats go by, he says, "Fine. Whatever. I'll keep my mouth shut. But I'm not getting knee deep in whatever overdramatized situation you think is happening here. It's seven lives, Penn." He shrugs his shoulders as if he doesn't care. But the way he stares at me says otherwise.

"All life is precious. Why do you think I was banished because of *one*?"

Just then, Michaela bursts into the room.

"Penn. It's Kismet."

Nineteen

Michaela huffs and puffs as if she ran across the entire heavens to get to us. "I found her in the prison of souls! We have to save her."

"The what?" I ask.

Bending over, she braces herself on her knees, sending her blonde hair cascading on either side of her body. "The prison of souls," she pants out. "It's not supposed to exist, but someone's opened it. And she's trapped in there, along with Andrew and the other five. Penn. They didn't go to heaven, where I left them. Someone's kidnapped them in the worst possible way."

As she takes a deep breath, trying to slow her breathing, Michaela looks up at Webber. She shoots straight up. "Webber, I didn't see you there." Her tone is guarded.

"He found me here. We have no choice but to trust him, and him us. As he has so kindly reminded me, I'm fallen and have nothing to lose. I could destroy him just as easily as he could destroy me."

Michaela looks between us, a frown pulling at the corners of her mouth. But I can't tell which one of us has met with her disapproval, maybe both.

She approaches the two of us, her frown still in its place. Her presence is suddenly not that of the welcoming, happy girl next door. She's an intimidating and formidable woman. We both stood up when she ran into the room, but seeing her like this is enough to make us sink back into our stools. "Listen, you two. I'm about sick of the pissing contest between you. I'm only going to say this once, and I'm not pleased that I have to say it at all. Get over yourselves. This isn't about you. This is about saving lives. Human lives. The lives that we've devoted the entirety of our existence to protect and care for." She clenches her fists at her sides as she speaks. I have never even seen her mad, let alone this angry.

I chance a glace at Webber, and he is totally cowed into submission, all but whimpering in his seat. Inwardly, I roll my eyes. Coward.

"Webber, either come with us or don't, but if I hear that you breathed a word about Penn to anyone at all, Penn won't be the only one you need to fear." Her blue eyes bore into him, and all he can do is nod.

"Penn, let's go." But as she turns to leave, she spots someone in the doorway.

Galenia stands there with an open mouth, tears pooling in her eyes. "Penn," she breathes.

The sight of her washes over me like a warm breeze, and a smile tugs at my lips as I whisper her name. "Galenia." She runs to my open arms, and we hold each other tight.

"Well, this is a nice love fest," Webber says, interrupting our moment.

Galenia ignores him completely. "What are you doing here?" Fear clouds her joyful expression. "If they find you—"

I cut her off. "It's Kismet. She's in trouble. And it's not just her. There are others. Something is happening."

She frowns as she considers my words.

"What are you doing here?" I ask her.

"I thought I heard voices."

"From your quarters?" I ask.

"No, I was out walking. I couldn't sleep, and anyway, it's nearly time to start the day. There's a lot of uncertainty around here lately. It's not something a Fate deals with real well," she says as she looks at Webber. "As I'm sure you well know."

Webber seems to shrink back into his chair. "I'm sorry," he says quietly. I'm pretty sure Galenia is the only person Webber would ever willingly apologize to.

"Horatia will want to help too."

"Too?" I ask. "No. I don't want to get you involved. You don't need to endanger yourselves."

"Penn," Michaela says sternly, "we need all the help we can get."

I sigh and nod, giving Galenia the go ahead to retrieve Horatia.

While we wait, I sort through my questions. "What is the prison of souls, Michaela?"

"The humans refer to it as purgatory—a place where souls would go before their ultimate place in the heavens is decided. The problem was that they could stay there indefinitely. It was unnatural. A soul needs a home, a place, even if it's hell. Plus, those who ran the prison were… unsavory. They tended to go outside their duties to punish the souls inside. So, centuries upon centuries ago, the prison was sealed, although many of the humans still thought it existed. To be trapped in there is a fate worse than death."

"Punish?" I ask. I don't like the sound of that, especially not when Andrew and Kismet are caught in there.

"Try not to think about it." Her grim expression says enough for the time being.

"So who could have opened it now? Who would even be capable of doing such a thing?" Webber asks.

"Aside from God, I don't know. And since He was the one who closed it in the first place, I can't see Him reopening it. The demons who run the outer gates of Hell don't have the resources or the intelligence for something like that. Their jobs are simply to keep those who belong inside, and those who don't out. They're the ones I found wandering closest to the prison."

"So, if God is capable of closing the prison, why not take this to Him? I think He could wrap this up in a nice little pack-age for us," Webber persists.

I think about what he said to me before I was dismissed. That there might be more work for me to do, and He's not through with me. "Maybe He's using us to do just that," I say, and Michaela smiles and nods.

"How did you even find it?" I ask.

She sighs. "Normally, I don't go past the gates. In both cases, guardians are there to collect the souls, be it heavenly angels or demons. When the guardians aren't there for heaven, it's not as big a deal. I just lead them through the gate and go. My last surprise was Kismet. And the guardians weren't there," she says sadly.

"This last soul was different too, and not just because he was going to hell. No one showed up to take him either. He fought me, of course, but I wrestled him inside and offloaded him on one of the demons on the outskirts. After giving the gatekeeper a stern talking to, I turned to leave. I mean, we're overwhelmed here. The last thing I need is for the guardians to not do their jobs." She sighs, trying to compose herself. "Anyway, I've only been on the other side of the gates a few times. Once, when I first became a Reaper, they took us through hell to show us what happens to the humans there. They did the same thing for heaven. As a Reaper, empathy is important. So, anyway, I knew to expect the moaning, screaming, and crying. But something felt off. It was too loud considering it was so far from the belly of hell. So I followed the sound and found the prison." She visibly shivers, as if what she saw there has affected her to her core.

I'm devastated in a way I didn't think was possible. The losses I experienced on Earth shattered me. But knowing my dear friends are tortured souls is so much worse. I fight the urge to let it overwhelm me. Now's the time for action, and I let my anger kill my sadness and fuel the need to move, to do something.

"I'm not sure what's worse. The souls I saw trapped there or the empty shackles lined up on the walls. There were so many empties." She pauses and looks up at me, her eyes filled with a fear so basic, it gives me chills. "This isn't over, Penn. Not by a long shot."

We stare at each other for a few moments when Michaela jumps a little. "I almost forgot." She pulls a letter and a small package from a pocket I didn't know her dress had. "It's from Fia. I really like her," Michaela says with a smile.

Penn,

I'm so glad Michaela found you. Didn't I tell you she would? We are all fine here on Earth. Cedric is reluctantly carrying on. You actually inspired him to hire a designer. He says she's not nearly as good as you, but she's good in her own way. Aida and Cody have welcomed me into their circle, and I've assured them all you are well. I told them you're just off sowing your wild oats, or licking your wounds. I forget which one. At any rate, please, do not worry about us.

Now is the time to focus on the task at hand. There's more at stake here than just a few lives. I can feel it. The winds are changing, Penn. Keep them at your back, or you'll be swept away, and the rest of us will follow.

Although my fate is here on Earth, a place I know you hold near and dear to your heart as much as I do, Fate has something bigger in store for you. I'm sure of it.

Enjoy a cookie from Aida. You're lucky I didn't eat it. She did send a whole batch for you, but some of them got lost in transit. Hopefully, Michaela has better luck with the delivery process. They are delicious.

All my best.

—Fia

I shake my head. It's the perfect mix of sarcasm, comfort, and advice. Perfectly Fia.

Just as I'm enjoying the cookie and rereading her note again, Horatia bursts into the room and grabs me in a big bear hug. I return the hug and spin her around.

"I thought I'd never see you again," she says through tears.

"Me too."

"So, what's the plan?" she asks, always ready to take action.

"To save Kismet and the others," I answer.

We stand in a circle looking at each other, five heavenly beings not sure of the future. Are we enough to save her and all of humanity from their fates?

Michaela takes my right hand, and Galenia takes my left. Surprisingly, even Webber joins in.

"So now what? We sing Kumbaya?" Webber asks.

We all chuckle. I don't know if we'll be enough to save my world. But I know we'll either succeed or die trying. And that's more than enough for me.

ERICKSON

NAMES

Abaddon: Destruction. Notorious Watcher

Aida: Helper. Cody's wife and brother to Cedric.

Amedia: Brazen or shameless. Aida's sister.

Andrew: Warrior or strength. Kismet's true love.

Cassandra: Prophetess. Kareena's doll.

Cedric: War leader or gift of splendor. Aida's brother and owner of Feldman's Bridal.

Pearl: Precious stone. One of the names that pops up while Penn is with the Reapers.

Cody: Helpful. Aida's husband, who helps Penn out of the swamp.

Columbus: Curious. Cody and Aida's only boy.

Eve: Lively or life. Cody and Aida's oldest (and first) daughter.

Fia: Weaver. The woman that Penn replaced as Spinner.

Frederico: Peaceful. One of the names that pops up while Penn is with the Reapers.

Galenia: Small and intelligent. The third Fate who decides how a life will end.

Horatia: Timekeeper. The second Fate who decides how long a life will be.

Jeff: Peaceful. One of the names that pops up while Penn is with the Reapers.

Kareena: Innocent and pure. Cody and Aida's youngest daughter.

Kismet: Destiny. Andrew's true love.

Marshal: From the marsh. The airboat driver.

Michaela: Feminine of Michael, the angel of death. The Reaper.

Nysa: New beginning. The first surprise name, the first to have her thread cut short.

Penn: Masculine form of Penelope, meaning Weaver. First of the three Fates, the Spinner.

Sandi: Defender or helper. The waitress who takes over Kismet's tables when Penn arrives at the diner.

Shiloh: Hebrew name meaning "the one to whom it belongs." The young boy Nysa cares for before she dies.

Webber: Weaver. Penn's rival who's promoted to Spinner when Penn is banished.

Meanings found using basic Google searches and Meaningof-Names.com

Did you enjoy this book?
Be sure and leave a review!

ACKNOWLEDGEMENTS

A brand-new series. After working on Unseen for so long, it's alternately fun and terrifying to start a new series. But of course, I didn't do it on my own.

First of all, thanks always go to God. I can't believe I've been so blessed as to pursue my dream this way. Writing is something I've wanted to do since I was in third grade. This is my seventh published book, and I still can't believe it. Thank You so much for letting this be my life. I am forever grateful.

This book is exciting for my husband and me as we push harder and harder to make this venture successful by our standards. My rock never fails to be endlessly supportive, and constantly come up with new ways to get out there and be seen. Hon, I have lifelong feelings of affection for you.

My editors worked harder than ever to make this turd shine, and I love them for it. Angela and Cynthia, you guys are amazing. Thank you so much for pouring yourselves, your time, and your efforts, into me and my books—no matter how annoying I can be with my questions about POV and tiny tweaks to my synopsis. You're worth your weight in gold, and chocolate.

Joanna, my favorite writing partner and true friend: You really helped me shape this book into what it is, and for that I'm so grateful. Our endless brainstorming sessions were invaluable to me. You deserve dinner with JT after this one.

My friends and family are my constant cheerleaders. They listen to me panic when things start crumbling, and they listen to my excited chatter about some new plot twist they don't even understand because they haven't read the book yet (because I'm still writing it). I'm a lot to take. I'm loud, active, overbearing, tactless, and a bit of a tornado when I get riled up. And somehow, I still have all these people who fiercely love me. Thanks guys. I certainly couldn't do this without you. (Mom, that means you…and Dad too, since he'll be mad I mentioned you and not him.)

Lastly, my deepest thanks to you, dear reader. As my daughter, my husband and I get older, I've come to value my time more and more. And you have chosen to spend yours with me. I will be forever grateful for that. I hope you enjoyed yourself as much as I did.

Until next time, happy reading, and I'll see you in March.

—S

ABOUT THE AUTHOR

Stephanie Erickson is an English Literature graduate from Flagler College. She lives in Florida with her family. The Fate is her seventh novel.

She loves to connect with readers! Follow her on Facebook at http://www.facebook.com/stephmerickson, Twitter @ sm_erickson, or stop by her Web site at www.stephanieerickson-books.com.

You can also get the latest news on new releases, contests, and author appearances by signing up for her newsletter on her Web site.

STEPHANIE'S BOOKS

Standalones:
The Blackout
The Cure

The Unseen Trilogy:
Unseen
Unforgiven
Undivided

The Dead Room Trilogy:
The Dead Room

The Children of Wisdom:
The Fate
The Reaper: Coming March 2016